FILTHY
Beautiful Lust

Filthy Beautiful Lies, Volume 3
By Kendall Ryan

Cover Design by Helen Williams of All Booked Out

Editing by Ellie of LoveNBooks

About the Book

Pace Drake loves sex. He knows where get it, what to say, what to do, and he makes no apologies for satisfying his needs. But when he meets single mom, Kylie Sloan, he's enthralled by her, and begins to question his standard operating procedure. After all, there's no chase, no mystery when banging a woman in a nightclub bathroom. Kylie's depth and determination make the sloppy, drunken hookups that fill his weekends seem empty and shallow. She's the opposite of the desperate, clingy women he's used to. She doesn't want or need anyone to take care of her and that only makes him want to care for her more.

Kylie's trust in men has vanished. The last guy she was with played ding-dong-ditch-it with her uterus and left her with a baby to raise. Now her infant son is the only man she has time for, even if she misses sex and intimacy more than she'd ever admit. Opening her heart up to a younger man who's best known for no-strings-attached sex and his casual lifestyle is probably the worst idea she's ever had. But Pace wants to prove to her there are still a few good guys left, and watching the sweet way he interacts with her baby makes her want to try...but she can really trust that his days of hitting it and quitting it are in his past?

Chapter One

The blonde on my arm is driving me nuts. If it weren't for her giant fake tits, that I very much want to play with later, I would have ditched her at the door.

We're at a fancy gala for Colton's charity, and the five thousand dollar a plate dinner is designed to bring in the last of the donations needed to ensure the school and hospital he plans to open are fully funded in the years to come. It's a great cause. But all I want to do is leave.

"Pace," my date says, tugging on my tuxedo-clad elbow. "Which one is your brother again?"

The one that looks exactly fucking like me, I want to answer. Instead, I point straight ahead to where Colton is standing talking with a group of benefactors. "Right there in the center. That's Colton. And his fiancé Sophie is beside him."

We've been mistaken for twins numerous times. He's three years older, but we share many similar features – tall stature, dark hair, deep blue eyes. The main difference – where Colton is hard edges and serious expressions – I'm friendly, open and relaxed. Life is too damn short to take so seriously. But apparently, grasping our similarities is beyond the capabilities of her three brain cells.

"Are you going to introduce me?" she asks.

She wants to meet my family? No. But rather than provide her with an answer she doesn't want to hear, I choose that moment to take a swig of my bourbon and pretend I didn't hear her.

I'd invited Sheena here tonight after meeting her at my health club. I didn't want to come to Colton and Sophie's big event alone and thought it might be nice to have someone to talk to over dinner. Unfortunately the only thing Sheena wanted to discuss was her recent *enhancements* and how the plastic surgeon convinced her to go to a bigger cup size and how she thought he only wanted to sleep with her.

Well no shit he wanted to fuck you sweetheart. *Line forms to the left, gentleman.*

After enduring two hours with the date from hell, all I want to do is fuck her in my car, and drop her off at home. *Classy, I know.* But you try spending ten thousand dollars on dinner for the world's most annoying date. I deserve a blow job at the very least.

Something tells me that on Monday I'll be looking for a new health club…

I've changed gyms six times this year. The cancellation fees are killing me. Maybe it's time to rethink my pick up strategy. *Nah.* There are lots of places in town with treadmills and free weights, and I have no problem switching clubs just to avoid running into my former hookups.

"Let's get you another champagne," I say, steering her toward the bar.

Once Sheena is situated on a bar stool, I slip away, making an excuse to use the men's room. Instead I head straight for where Sophie and Kylie are talking across the room.

My brother's fiancé, Sophie Evans, looks great tonight. Long silky dress, jewels at her throat and her hair is twisted up in some type of knot. She looks happy.

"Hey, sis," I greet her with a kiss to the back of her hand.

I won't treat her any differently after her sister's passing, because I know she wouldn't want it, but I do try to be sweet to her. After everything she's been through, she didn't break, and I'm so thankful. Colton needs a strong woman, and Sophie is the perfect complement to him. I don't plan to settle down anytime soon, but one day I hope to find a girl as good as Sophie. I still think his story about how they met and why she'd moved in was bullshit, but it didn't really matter. Colt was a lucky guy, and he knew it.

"Hi, Pace." Sophie grins up at me.

Next I turn to Kylie, who I've been trying to figure out for the past several months. She works for my brother, running the office operations for his charity, and I'm pretty sure she's responsible for tonight's gala. She's stunning – in a deep purple gown that flows beautifully over her curves, fiery auburn hair that falls in loose waves over her shoulders and brilliant green eyes that sparkle on mine. The way she watches me sends tingles shooting down my body, pulsing in my groin. My cock begins to swell. *What the fuck?* She's exquisite and classy and put together. The complete fucking opposite of my date.

"It's a great event. Congratulations," I lift her hand to my mouth and whisper against the back of it while watching her eyes.

She flinches at the contact and tugs her hand back, but treats me to a kind smile. "Thank you, Pace." The tone of her warm voice wrapping around my name is fucking sinful. I want to hear her moan out my name when she climaxes, I want to see her green eyes darken with lust, and watch her completely come apart beneath me.

I know she's a single mom, and I should just steer clear. She's nothing like the women I typically date, but something about her hypnotizes me.

"Where's your date?" Sophie asks.

"I'm not sure," I lie. I can see her from the corner of my eye, she's still at the bar and seems to be chatting it up with the bartender. Good. Maybe I can offload her on him tonight. I wouldn't mind going home instead with the elegant and sophisticated beauty I see before me.

"I was hoping to meet her," Sophie says.

Sophie doesn't understand there's a reason I've never introduced her to any of the women I'm seeing. They're all temporary. And besides, I doubt they'd hit it off. Sophie's interests go a little deeper than nail polish and handbags. My brother chose well.

"Isn't that the woman you were with?" Kylie asks, pointing across the room.

I follow her gaze to Sheena.

Fuck.

Sheena is currently bent backwards over the top of the bar. Her tits are practically hanging out, and she's letting the bartender pour shots of tequila down her throat.

Christ. This isn't a college frat party. It's an exclusive black-tie affair for millionaires and politicians and the nation's leading entrepreneurs. We're here for an important cause, not to get wasted and dance on the damn bar. But something tells me my date doesn't get that.

I don't often feel embarrassed, and shit, I love to cut loose and have fun as much as anyone, but this is not the time, nor the place. My face flushes slightly and I clench my jaw.

I like a woman who knows how to handle herself – someone poised and put together when she needs to be and freaky as hell in between the sheets. My eyes find Kylie's and something tells me she'd be that kind of woman.

"Yeah, Sheena's fun," I say, clenching my fists in an attempt to hide my true feelings.

Kylie frowns. "I introduced myself to her earlier, and she said her name was Trina."

"Shit. Is it?" I rub a hand through my hair. The look in her eyes tells me this is a piece of information I should have known.

Sophie excuses herself a moment later, and I'm thankful for the private moment with Kylie.

"Can I get you something else to drink?" I offer, tossing her a flirty grin.

Her answering smile is coy, guarded. "Shouldn't you be getting back to your date?"

A quick look over my shoulder at Sheena, or Trina, or whoever the hell she is, tells me I have no desire to spend any more time with her. In contrast to the beautiful woman standing before me, my date is all but forgotten. I might have thought she was sexy before, but now, I'm seeing her more clearly. Her dress is too short and her breasts are too big, even for my sizeable hands, while Kylie, in comparison, is perfectly proportioned—soft and curvy—just like a woman should be. I wouldn't mind devoting hours to exploring the valleys of her body. With my tongue. And my cock. The bastard throbs at the thought.

"She looks pretty well taken care of right now," I remark.

The bartender is all but ignoring the other customers in his eagerness to talk to her. He can have her for all I care. *Good luck, buddy.*

Kylie sets down her empty wine glass on the tray of a passing waiter. "I'm actually not much of a drinker. A glass of wine or two is generally my limit."

Good to know. I file that information away. Remembering her kid, I ask about him. "Where's Max tonight?"

She smiles lightly as though thinking about her baby brightens her mood. I like that, and I don't have a frigging clue why. "His nanny stayed late tonight. I'm sure he's in bed by now."

I still recall that day in the pool last summer when I'd taken the crying baby from her and entertained him all afternoon. I couldn't even be sure why I'd done it. I suppose, looking back, she just looked like she could use a hand. I've never liked seeing a woman struggle. Although a damsel in distress, she is not. I get the sense she's not the type to back down from a challenge and has enough strength and determination to succeed at just about anything she tried. A sexy quality, to be sure.

As we stand there, me sipping my bourbon, and Kylie grinning politely at the crowd, the silence between us grows. I feel like we have nothing in common, and I'm at a loss, trying to think of something to say, anything that will keep this beauty in my presence. There are so many things I want to know about her, but none of them are any of my goddamn business. How she tastes, what noises she makes when she comes. I also want to know how she ended up a single mother, and if Max's dad is still in the picture. I tried asking Colton about it once, but he remained incredibly vague. The asshat. If there was a worst wingman award, it would go to my brother.

"Have dinner with me this week," I say. It wasn't what I'd been planning to say, but once the words leave my mouth, they feel right.

"Pace, that's sweet of you to ask, but I can't..." She pauses, like she wants to say more, but doesn't. Her body language is all wrong too. Where women are normally vying to get closer, placing their hand on my bicep, or even brushing their breasts against my arm, Kylie stands straight and tall, like she wants to avoid physical contact at all costs.

"Are you here with someone?" I ask. It's also absolutely none of my business, but I'd happily shell out ten grand just to find out if she's fucking someone.

"No," she confirms.

"No boyfriend?" I press further. I need to know what I'm up against.

"There's been no one since Max's father," she says quietly.

My inner alpha male beats on his chest in triumph. "That's quite a dry spell."

"Indeed," she murmurs.

"It's just dinner, Kylie. It's not like I'm offering to step in and play daddy." I treat her to a playful, crooked smile, my dimple out in full force. I've heard it's quite irresistible and that's what I'm banking on.

"That's exactly why I can't. I'm sorry."

Fuck. Why am I such a fucking idiot?

"Oh," I stammer, at a loss for words for the first damn time in my life. *Christ. Grow a pair, Pace.*

"Besides, something tells me if you're interested in a woman like that," Kylie tips her chin toward the bar where Sheena, or Trina, is making a spectacle of herself, "you can't possibly be interested in a woman like me."

Hold the fuck on. Now that's where she's wrong. "Why's that?" I ask, meeting her fiery green gaze. If she's about to criticize herself, I will not hold back in proving to her how very wrong she is.

"Pace," she admonishes. "Look at her. They look…inflatable."

When I realize she's not tearing herself down, but instead chastising my taste in women, I almost want to laugh. "A woman like that is good for only one thing and we both know it," I say.

She raises her eyebrows, waiting for me to explain.

"One good fuck," I continue.

"You're crass." Her eyes light up, and her mouth twitches in an attempt not to smile.

"I'm direct, and you like it."

She shrugs. "At least you're honest. That's more than I can say for most men."

"Go out with me. One time, Kylie. What do you have to lose?"

I can practically see the wheels turning in her head, and for one brief, beautiful moment I think I might have a chance. "Bye Pace." She turns and walks away, her long legs carrying her across the room while my heart throbs.

Fuck.

"Kylie, wait."

She turns and tosses me a sexy wink. "Go have fun with Malibu Barbie.

This is not over.

I play to win.

Chapter Two

KYLIE

This is not my real life.

My real life is not evening gowns and silk panties and fancy dinners. It's heating bottles up at two a.m., spit-up stains on my yoga pants and fishing Cheerios out from between my couch cushions. But it feels amazing to pretend, if only for a brief moment.

As I sit in the back of the limousine Colton insisted I take, I remove my earrings one at a time and drop them into my handbag. The twinkling city lights blur past as we cruise down the freeway, and my thoughts drift back to the gala. The event had turned out beautifully, even better than I could have expected. But of course it isn't the details of the fundraiser occupying my brain. It's a certain six-foot, two-inch, well-muscled slice of man named Pace Drake. My boss's younger brother. And there is no way he'd be interested in the real me.

I chuckle to myself, remembering that he didn't even know his date's name. I should feel outraged that he all but ignored her in favor of paying me compliments and asking me out. Instead I'm strangely flattered. When a man as handsome as Pace paid you attention it felt wonderful. Especially for someone like me. He could have any woman he wanted. And for some strange reason he'd set his sights on me – with my post-pregnancy body that is still curvier than I would have liked.

But I'd shot him down, which I know is for the best. I have personal experience with men like him. They're looking for no-strings sex. And considering the last guy I was with played ding-dong-ditch-it with my uterus, and left me with a baby to raise, I'm more than a teensy bit skeptical about men like him.

Max is the only man I have time for these days. And the only man I will give my heart to.

I can't resist pulling out my iPhone to look at the pictures of Max. Just as I know I won't be able to resist going into his room to listen to the sounds of him breathing and leaning down to his crib to smell his baby scent, even though I know there's a chance it'll wake him. But his chunky baby thighs and big round tummy are too much for this mama to resist.

It was actually quite sweet of Pace to ask about Max. Last summer, the first time I'd met Pace at Colton's pool party, he carted a screaming, teething Max around all that afternoon, swimming with him in the pool and bouncing him in his big arms. Colton seemed to have no explanation for Pace's sudden interest in the baby. I was convinced it was merely him taking pity on his brother's employee. I was beyond stressed out when Max was cutting his first two teeth. And I'm sure I looked it.

As flattered as I am about his interest in me, I'm fine with being celibate and focusing on my career and being a mom. Well, that's not *entirely* true. I do miss having a man in my life. I miss strong arms holding me close, the brush of a stubbled cheek on mine, the feeling of absolute security. When I'm ready to start a relationship again, it will be with a man who makes me feel safe. There is nothing safe about Pace Drake.

He's as dangerous as they come. Young. Sexy. Wealthy. Carefree. The dark, hungry look in his eyes promised me hot, intense sex. I shiver, recalling the way my body responded under his watchful stare. Yes, I'm sure he'd be a wild beast in bed, probably with a giant cock to match his stamina, not that I will ever know such things.

As the limo driver pulls to a stop in front of my house, I push all the crazy thoughts from my head. Fantasies are nice, but it's time to get back to my real life.

Chapter Three

PACE

I haven't stopped thinking about her since Saturday night. No, not Malibu Barbie. I'd accepted her proffered blow job on the drive home – it was mediocre – and then dropped her off at her front door. I haven't heard from her since. Which is just as well, because it's Kylie I can't seem to get out of my brain.

I had no doubt she saw straight through me because that sassy mouth of hers had called me out on the one-night stand. I know there's no way we'd fit neatly into each other's worlds, but I have to try.

When I arrive at Colton's office just after lunchtime, I find him standing beside his assistant's desk, flipping through a stack of documents.

"Hey bro." I slap him on the back. "You have a minute for your favorite brother?"

He rises to his full height and frowns at me. "Do I have a choice?"

I roll my eyes. I know he doesn't like being interrupted during the work day. But too damn bad. I'd helped him with his woman plenty of times. "No. Now come on."

I let myself into his adjoining office and hear his footsteps behind me. I'm not usually one for midday drinks, but rather than sit down in one of the plush armchairs that provide the perfect view of the Los Angeles skyline, I head to his liquor cabinet. What the hell, I could use some loosening up. I've been wound as tight as a damn virgin since Kylie walked away from my invitation on Saturday night. Women didn't refuse me, and so to say I'm thrown off my game is putting it mildly.

"Want one?" I ask, removing a glass and the bottle of pricey bourbon from the cabinet.

Colton shakes his head. "What's going on, man? Everything okay?"

I take a sip of the liquor and immediately decide drinking is a bad idea. I'm already on edge and frustrated. The alcohol will only make me obsess more. Abandoning the glass, I sit down in a leather chair across from him and let out a heavy sigh. "Tell me about Kylie."

His gaze narrows. "Fuck no. You and Kylie?" He shakes his head, rising to his feet. "No. Abso-fucking-lutely not. If this is what you came here to talk to me about, you can leave now." He points to the door, his expression unwavering.

Goddamn. "You're no fun." Changing my mind, I stride over to the cabinet, grab the glass and down the rest of the drink. It burns like a motherfucker on the way down, but it'll do the trick, numbing whatever this weird sensation is inside my chest.

"I'm serious, Pace. She's a good girl. She doesn't need to get tangled up in your…ways…"

"My ways?" Now I'm getting pissed. He's saying I'm not good enough for her.

"Hit it and quit it. Pump and dump. Whatever you want to call it, it's not happening. Not with Kylie."

"I know that, asshole. I wanted to take her out – like legitimately take her out to dinner. Enjoy her company."

He frowns at me again, that crease in his forehead deepening. "You're telling me you don't want to fuck her?"

"Don't be a dumbshit. Of course I want to fuck her. But I'm just saying that I wouldn't hit it once and never call her again."

"What would you do, then? Move in? Marry her? Raise her son?" he challenges.

"I haven't thought that fucking far ahead. Christ." Now I'm pacing the floor of his office and I have no idea why. This entire exchange is stressing me out. I came here hoping to get her number, and instead I'm getting grilled like a steak. He's pulling the older brother card on me like he does so often. *The dick.*

"And that's exactly why I don't want you messing around with her. You don't have a plan. Kylie needs a man with a plan. Not one with an agenda that only includes getting his crank yanked."

I sink down into the chair, hating this concerned sibling act he's got down to a science.

"Kylie needs someone ready for a serious relationship. That isn't you, and this isn't a good idea, and we both know it."

"Just like it wasn't a good idea for you to marry the mega-bitch Stella. But you didn't listen to me. You had to find out for yourself." His fists clench at his sides. He hates it when I bring up his ex. Too damn bad.

"You didn't forget about our engagement party this Saturday, did you?"

"Of course not," I answer. I'd totally forgotten it was this weekend. Good thing Collins and I had already gone in on a gift. "Where's it at again? The Beverly Hills Country Club?" I smirk. His last engagement party was there.

Colton growls out an expletive, apparently not appreciating my sarcastic sense of humor. "No dipshit. Nothing fancy and over the top. This is Sophie, remember?"

Sophie. Of course I remember. She is nothing like his first wife, thank God. That evil bitch would have eaten your balls for breakfast if you weren't careful. I cup my nuts, remembering her and shudder.

"It's at the house. Six o'clock. We're grilling and playing yard games," Colton finishes.

"Will Kylie be there?" I smirk.

"Get the fuck out," he hisses, tossing his stapler at me on my way out the door. It hits the wall with a dull thud, and I know I'm back in the game.

***

On Saturday afternoon, I'm seated on the diving board, dangling my bare feet in the pool waiting for the party to begin. Sophie and Colton are standing in the backyard, greeting guests as they arrive, accepting congratulations and showing off her engagement ring. There's still no sight of Kylie. As the days passed, I started to question why my focus was so singularly on this woman. But then I see her, and it all comes rushing back.

She's wearing a white, gauzy sundress with sandals on her feet. Her hair is tied back into a simple ponytail. She's stunning. There is something so natural and simple about her. I cannot look away. My eyes wander down her bare legs. They are toned and tanned nicely. I wonder if she's a runner. Her hand is outstretched and a chubby baby toddles alongside her, holding on to her finger.

It's been a while since I've seen the little guy – I didn't realize he'd be walking now. I continue watching them from my perch on the diving board.

Kylie leads him over to the bride and groom-to-be, then lifts him into her arms, doling out hugs and well-wishes, though I'm not close enough to hear what is being said.

When I see Collins arrive with our dad, I hop off the diving board, the bottom cuffs of my khaki pants wet, and cross the patio.

"Hey old man," I greet him with a thump on the back.

"Pace Alexander." He grins at me and pulls me into a hug.

It's been way too long since I've seen him. The Christmas before last, I think. I'm pretty sure he has a new, young girlfriend keeping him busy. He still works, but we're all on him to retire. That way he could spend more time out here in LA with all of us. And I'm sure Colton and Sophie are going to start popping out kids soon enough.

"What's her name?" I ask him.

"Who?"

"You look way too fit and happy. There's gotta be a woman."

He gives me a sly smile and looks from me, to Collins and back again. "I plead the fifth."

"Just tell me she's older than me at least."

"How old are you again?"

"Twenty-five," I say.

"Don't worry about it, son. Now point me in the direction of this lovely Sophie I've heard so much about."

Collins and I lead him across the yard to meet his future daughter-in-law. Sophie wins my dad over instantly, which is really no surprise. She's sweet, kind, down to earth and easy to get along with. As we chat and make small talk with the family my eyes keep straying to Kylie. She's holding Max against her chest as they twirl around in the grass, his squeals of joy audible even from here. I get a strange look from Colton when he catches me watching them. I decide to go now, while he's busy with Dad, and before he can interfere. *The cock-blocking asshole.*

Since Max is the only child here, and Colton's home isn't exactly kid-friendly, Kylie's brought her own toys for him to play with. *Smart.* They've already littered the yard with trucks and balls in various sizes and colors.

When I get closer, Max is pushing a green tractor toward her with chubby outstretched hands.

"Raising him up right, I see." I nod toward the John Deere tractor her son is driving.

She looks up at me and smirks. "I didn't know you were familiar with anything outside of BMW and Mercedes."

She's called me out and she doesn't even know it. I drive a BMW M3. "A man can still appreciate fine machinery." I sink to the ground on bended knees. "It's all about the details. See?" I lift up the secret hatch under the seat.

Max begins to clap as I drop a couple blades of grass into the hatch and close it once again. He's delighted to sit here in the grass, opening and closing the new found secret compartment while I talk to the beautiful girl in front of me.

Kylie sinks to ground, and crosses her legs, since she's in a dress. We sit in silence for a few minutes, just watching him play.

Her son doesn't look like her. He must get his olive skin tone, and dark hair from his father. But his mannerisms are all her. The way he breaks into a wide smile and squeals with delight reminds me of her own bright smile and hearty laughter. The way he stands and surveys his surroundings with a curious expression is Kylie's too. They're both so calm and grounded and there's something I like about that.

"Do you want something to drink?" Kylie does some type of sign-language to him as she speaks and a moment later, he repeats the move back to her. She hands him a blue plastic sippy cup from inside her bag. He brings it to his mouth and tilts his head so far back that he falls into the grass and just lays there, drinking like he's been travelling through the desert and deprived of liquid. I crack a smile. While he lies there quietly, I take a moment to look at Kylie. To really look at her.

The sun brings out her hair's reddish undertone. Her skin looks incredibly soft and her mouth is full and has a natural pout that women spend thousands to achieve via plastic surgery.

Her bare shoulders are delicate and tanned. Sticky fingers reach out for her, and she doesn't hesitate, lifting him into her arms and letting him plaster her cheeks with wet kisses. I wouldn't know what that felt like – to have a little body clinging to me and so happy just to be near me. Watching her interact with her baby, it's hard to look away.

Max tosses down his juice cup and wanders from her lap to where I'm sitting. "Hi buddy," I say, meeting his intense stare. He's silently watching me, but I can see the wheels turning in his little head. He's trying to piece together who I am and what I'm doing. *I like your mom, little dude, so be cool.* Holding out my hand, I ask him if he can give me five and he does, smacking his sticky palm against mine with a squeal. Then he lunges toward me and begins climbing me like a tree.

"Max, don't do that..." Kylie reaches for him, but I wave her off.

"He's fine. Unless you're not okay with this?"

She opens, then closes her mouth, thinking it over. "No, it's fine. He doesn't often play with men, so I think this might be good for him. I'm just happy he's not shy. I've been waiting for that stage to hit."

I look down into giant bright blue eyes. "You're not afraid of me, are you buddy?"

He squeals and slaps a chubby palm against my face. Okay then, that settles that.

I spend the next fifteen minutes flying him like an airplane around the yard, hunting for frogs in the garden and letting him dip his fingers into the pool while I hold onto him.

Kylie watches everything with a neutral expression that makes me wish I knew what she was thinking. And even though she mingles a bit and greets the other guests, her eyes are never far from us.

Once Max tires of me, he reaches for her. "Mumma," he says in a little gravelly voice.

I place him in her arms, my hands sliding against her bare shoulder as we make the exchange. Her skin is warm and petal soft and her eyes dart up to mine. "Thank you."

"Anytime," I say, sticking my hands into my pockets. Without that wiggly little body in my arms, they feel a bit useless just dangling there at my sides.

The photographer Colton and Sophie hired to capture the memories of their engagement party approaches. "Will you three get together for a picture?"

Kylie stiffens, and I see her mouth open like she's about to refuse the photographer.

"It's just a photo," I remind her. She's desperate to refuse anything that could be construed as intimate between us. "Please," I add.

Kylie settles Max on her hip so they're both facing the camera and I toss my arm around her shoulder, hugging them both, and smile brightly at the photographer.

She takes a few shots and then lowers her camera. "What an adorable baby you two have."

"Oh, he's not..." I pause, mentally smacking myself. I'd been about to deny him as mine– and he's not–but I suddenly realize that I wouldn't mind people thinking he was. I wouldn't mind someone assuming that this beautiful woman and her baby belong to me.

Kylie's eyes flash to mine, wondering why I haven't corrected the woman.

I shrug, lifting an eyebrow to tell her it's okay. Her brow crinkles and she chews on her lower lip, but doesn't say anything, instead turning her attention back to Max.

In the distance I see the caterers setting out platters of food at the long banquet table on the patio. "Shall we get something to eat?"

"Sure," she says, then makes the sign for *eat* to Max, which he eagerly imitates.

Chapter Four

KYLIE

Pace and I are seated at one of the banquet tables dressed in white linens with Max between us. I'm nervous he's going to spill something or ruin the tablecloth with his enthusiastic method of eating, but Pace only smiles adoringly at him. It makes me feel unsure and on edge.

I share a plate of food with Max, and he nibbles on grilled salmon, potatoes and cucumber salad like a champ. I'm thankful I don't have a picky eater. Otherwise, it'd be Cheerios for dinner, because that was all I packed. Of course I also forgot to put on his bib, which meant half of the food was ending up on his shirt. I'll be changing him into his jammies after this.

Pace looks on, clearly impressed by Max's ability to shovel fistfuls of food into this mouth. "Does he have any teeth in there?"

"He has four."

"How old is he?" he asks next.

I don't know what's up with his sudden interest in my child, or maybe it's just that he's trying to be polite and make small talk since he's stuck sitting next to the lady with the baby. "He turned one last month."

"So it's just you and him?" The depth of Pace's expression surprises me. There's usually a crooked grin on his lips, a dimple peeking from one cheek, and a mischievous sparkle in his eyes. Now there's only a set mouth, strong jawline and deep blue eyes watching me, waiting for my response.

I swallow a lump in my throat. I don't need anyone. At least that's what I tell myself. But Max... I feel bad for my son. I hate to think about when he's older having to explain to him that his own father wanted nothing to do with him. "It's just us," I say, my voice going tight. I take a sip of water and exhale deeply. "Where's your girlfriend tonight?"

"I don't have a girlfriend."

"What about the blonde from the other weekend?"

"She was a one-time thing."

"Classy." I raise an eyebrow at him. He's blunt, but for some reason I like his direct style of communication and the way his eyes never stray from mine. He doesn't make excuses, doesn't try to cover up who he is. Or what that night had been – it was a one-time hookup. God, I don't even remember what that'd be like.

I might be a mom now, but my body still has needs, yearnings...that I promptly ignore. Yes, sir, I shut those feelings down with a vice clamp. They are dangerous and make me want things that just aren't possible for me right now.

"I still want to take you to dinner," he says, reading my faraway thoughts.

"We're having dinner," I point out and feed another bite to Max from the end of my fork, hoping to actually get some of the food in his mouth this time.

Pace stares straight ahead, looking out at the ocean, and for the first time, I begin to wonder what he's thinking, what he sees when he looks at me. He's a handsome, eligible bachelor. Surely his prospects are better than a single mom so jaded it'd take a miracle for me to trust again. Though I have to admit, there is something in me that loved seeing him with Max. His big hands that curled all the way around Max's belly and ribcage, the gentle way he flew him through the air while Max giggled…Max deserves more moments like that. The rational side of my brain knows that, but I won't have him feel the loss and rejection when Pace decides a blond with inflatable breasts is more fun than a twenty-nine year old single mom and her son. And he was guaranteed to.

Men like him don't change overnight. I need to keep my feet firmly on the ground and my head out of the clouds, no matter how freaking cute he is.

After dinner, I change Max into his pajamas, we brush all four of his teeth and I read him the two books I'd packed. I know he's tired because he's tugging on his ears through the second book. It's his tell. A clear signal that he's ready to be laid down and won't get up again until morning. And it's a good thing too, because after twelve hours of playing and lifting him and carrying him my back is aching and I just want to sit down and relax for a minute or two before we have to drive home.

I spot Sophie and Colton by the outdoor fireplace.

"Hey guys." I lean in and give each of them a hug. "Great party. Thank you for having us." I feel bad that I haven't spent any time with the hosts yet, but chasing a one-year-old around keeps you busy.

Sophie's mouth curls in a smile. It's so good to see her happy. "You look gorgeous tonight."

I chuckle, realizing she usually only sees me dressed for work. And since I work at home, my ensemble usually consists of a pair of faded yoga pants and a stretched out t-shirt.

If I'm being honest, the only reason I took the extra time and care getting ready – wearing a sundress, curling my hair – was because I knew I'd see Pace again. It's stupid, and I brush off her compliment.

"Max is sleeping in your den. Hope that's okay," I say.

"Absolutely," Colton says. "You could have put him upstairs in a bed, you know?"

I wave him off. "He's fine. But thank you."

"Looks like he had fun with Pace today," Colton remarks, watching me closely to see my reaction. Colton and his brother are really quite different. Where Colton is intense, calculated and exacting in everything he does, Pace is open and easy going and puts a smile on your face, despite your best efforts to hate him.

I want to drill him for information, ask him what is up with Pace's attention toward me and my son, but I don't want to appear to be overly interested. "Just a couple more days until you guys set off, right?" I ask.

Colton wraps his arms around Sophie's middle and tugs her back against him. "It'll be Sophie's first time in Africa. The first of many, hopefully. I'm anxious to see all the progress from my visit there two years ago."

Colton and I discuss the logistics of their trip, while Sophie peppers us with questions of her own. They've each been receiving the necessary vaccinations before their travel, and have their passports and travel visas ready. They'll be gone for three weeks. I'll miss seeing Sophie on the days she works with me.

"I wish you could come, Kylie," Sophie says. "Would your nanny stay with Max?"

I shrug. "She probably would if I asked her, but I don't think I could handle being separated from Max for so long." He is my heart.

She nods like she understands. But I don't think she truly does. She will when she's a mother.

Pace wanders over in bare feet, his white shirtsleeves are pushed up, showing off tan and muscular forearms sprinkled with light hair. He's dangling a bottle of beer from one hand and grinning at me.

"Where's your mini?" he asks, looking directly at me.

My belly tightens. "He's all partied-out."

"Excuse us," Colton says. "We've got to go say goodnight to Dad. He's still operating on the eastern time zone." He leads Sophie away and I'm, once again, alone with Pace. I'm not sure why I feel so out of my element when I'm near him. It's probably because I don't understand his motivations, I decide.

"Care to join me by the water?" he asks.

"Sure." He leads me toward the beach. And even though my brain is screaming at me to say no, my feet carry me down toward the water, following closely behind him.

PACE

I lead Kylie to a secluded spot on the beach. After seeing her with the little koala bear she's had attached to her hip or by her side all afternoon, it's like part of her is missing. There's something I don't like about it.

"This okay?" I ask, indicating a dry spot in the sand where the tall grasses shield some of the wind blowing in off the water.

"Fine," she says, lowering herself down. "The monitor should still work out here." Kylie crosses her legs and folds her hands in her lap.

I sink down beside her. The sand is warm and sugar soft. The gentle sounds of the low rolling waves and moonlight gleaming down on us make a romantic backdrop. If she were any other woman, I would have her down on her knees by now with my cock deep in her throat. To be honest, I'm a bit at a loss right now, unsure what to do or say next. It's an interesting change for me.

"Did you enjoy yourself tonight?" I ask.

"Max had fun, so that was good."

It wasn't what I'd asked her, but I let it go.

When she talks about her son, her eyes light up and her mouth curves into a silly grin. It's actually quite adorable. She's a far cry from the women in my past. For one, she's not all over me, and two, she's mostly quiet and contemplative as she looks out at the water. She feels no need to fill the silence with nonsense jabber. It's refreshing.

She's never fake, never tries to impress me, she's just comfortable in her own skin and that makes the man inside me take notice.

From the corner of my vision, I watch the breeze lift the stray pieces of hair that have escaped her ponytail. They flutter around her neck and cheeks while Kylie looks straight ahead, watching the waves. I'm certain she has no idea how beautiful she is with her minimal makeup and no-fuss style. I was noticing things I never took the time to notice before, like the delicate scent hanging around her, and how soft and smooth her skin looked.

When you fuck a woman in the bathroom of a nightclub, there's no reason to take her out again. Where's the chase? The mystery? I liked to get a little crazy now and then, but I still believed a woman should behave like a woman. Kylie is every bit poised and put together with a shit ton of mystery and enough depth to make me want to give chase.

In Los Angeles her modesty is refreshing. She would be the type of woman to age gracefully. No injections or fillers or skin pulled too tight around her eyes. She'd still be beautiful at sixty. I could see it now. Long silver hair, the same cheeky gleam in her green eyes, as she pushed up on her toes to kiss her grown son on the cheek.

"I should go. It's late, and..."

Hell, I can't let her walk away yet. "Max's asleep inside, right?"

She looks down at the baby monitor in her hands. "Yes, but..."

"You could stay for a little while longer, couldn't you?"

She looks like she wants to say no, but then at the last minute, she surprises me. "I suppose so."

"I know you said you're not much of a drinker, but could I get you anything...water? Soda?"

"No, I'm fine. You didn't have to hang around us all night, Max and I, I mean," she says.

"I wanted to, Kylie."

She swallows and glances up at my eyes, trying to read if I'm feeding her a line. "Pace, I've worked for Colton for over a year now. He's told me a few stories about his younger brother. I know this isn't you. You're not the guy who's looking to settle down with a single mom. You said so yourself at the gala."

"Then what kind of guy am I, Kylie?"

Her brilliant emerald gaze flashes on mine, looking dark and dangerous. "You're the guy who drops panties and breaks hearts and does it all with a sultry grin. I've heard the stories. They're a bit wild." She winks.

I'm going to fucking kill Colton. I don't care that it's his engagement party. He's a dead man. Shit, I realize I can't do that to Sophie. I'll just have to come up with some type of plan B to make him pay.

"Unless you have some type of mommy dearest issue you need to explore?" she raises a brow.

Her joke is off color, but she doesn't know it. "I lost my mother when I was nine."

"Oh, God, I didn't know. I'm so sorry." Her hands flies to her chest and stays there while she watches me.

"It's okay. You didn't know."

"I'm sorry. Colton never mentioned it." Her tone is tender and caring.

I shrug. I'm not surprised. "It's not something we like to discuss."

As we sit here together in the company of the endless blue ocean, I can't help but wonder if my interest in Kylie has anything to do with the fact that I do see her as a mother. Her softness, the love I see pouring out of her in every interaction with Max – maybe those are things that attract me to her. Her warmth, her devotion – they are all part of what makes her beautiful. It doesn't take a psychiatrist to find the link here. But it isn't something I care to dwell on.

Beside me, Kylie cups handfuls of sand and lets them drift through her parted fingers like a sieve.

"Can I ask you something?" I ask.

She nods.

"What happened to Max's father?" It's something I've wondered about since the first time I met her, but I'm only brave enough to ask now, in the cover of night, and once she's already stumbled over the death of my mother.

She pauses her motions, letting the sand fall from her hands, then dusts them off. "Have you ever been in love, Pace?" she surprises me by asking.

"No."

"Never?"

"Nope." I'm hopeful that it'll happen someday, I just haven't gotten there yet. I've been too busy building my career and sleeping my way through the LA singles scene.

"It's a scary thing – handing your heart over like that. Giving someone the very best pieces of yourself." Her eyes are far away and she remains staring out at the water as she speaks. "I met Max's father, Elan, when I first moved to Los Angeles a few years ago. He was quite a bit older than me, thirty-six at the time, already settled and successful. I didn't know anyone in the city, and he seemed like a safe choice. We dated for about six months, and even though we never talked about our future in the terms of marriage and children, I felt like we were building toward something real and long-lasting. We stayed together every weekend, at either his place or mine. And even though we were careful – I was on birth control at the time – somehow, I got pregnant. I guess they're serious with those fine print warnings about no birth control method being one-hundred percent effective. I just never thought anything like that would happen to me."

The urge to reach over and take her hand in mine is nearly overwhelming. I fist my hands in my lap instead and wait for Kylie to continue.

"I was scared when I found out – mostly because it was so unexpected. I was just getting my career off the ground, and my relationship with Elan was still pretty new. I never thought I had to worry about being a single mom, though. I wasn't scared to tell Elan. He'd never been anything other than loving and kind toward me." Kylie's tone tightens at the end, like she has something stuck in her throat.

I hate the direction this story is headed and I hate myself even more for asking and making her relive all these bitter memories. I want to kick myself in the balls for my curiosity.

"I called him over to the apartment I lived in at the time, I didn't want to tell him over the phone. He came over, playful and curious about what it was that I wanted to say. But the moment the words, *I'm pregnant* left my lips, all playfulness evaporated. His entire demeanor changed. The kind side of him disappeared and was replaced with a man who was suddenly all business. He wanted to know when, how and what I planned to do about it. It took me several moments to understand he wasn't using the word *we*. He was asking about what *I* planned to do. I was on my own from that point forward, it was just me and the little life growing inside of me. I felt sick and hollow. He had put this baby inside me and now he suddenly wanted nothing to do with us. It was a harrowing feeling."

Kylie's quiet for a moment and there's no way in hell I'm probing any further, but I can tell this story is far from over. And I have a feeling it's going to get even more heart-wrenching before it gets better.

"Elan stopped calling, he stopped responding to my texts and emails. He cut all ties. When I was about six months pregnant, I ran into him at the drug store one night. I had a massive craving for ice cream and ventured out in my maternity pajamas to pick some up. I still cringe thinking about what I must have looked like to him." She shudders and buries her face in her hands.

Picturing her with a firm, round belly, I see nothing she should feel ashamed about. She's a gorgeous woman — and while I'm not typically attracted to pregnant women, Kylie with a baby growing inside of her makes my mouth curl into a dopey grin.

"I saw him and some young blonde piece of arm candy," she continues. "They were buying condoms at the checkout counter. His eyes slid from mine down to my rounded belly and back up again. He made some comment to the sales clerk about using condoms, even when a woman claims to be on birth control. And then he was gone. I hated myself for trusting him with my heart. I hated myself for still missing him. But the most painful thing of all came a few weeks later. His assistant delivered a check for fifty grand and the note inside said that he didn't want to be bothered with making weekly child support payments, and that I should use the money to start a college savings fund. Which, of course, I did – for Max's sake – even though I hated accepting that money from him. I've had no other contact with him," she finishes.

"What about when Max was born?" I can't understand a man who would just walk away from his woman and child – especially this woman. She is so strong and independent and stunningly beautiful.

"Nothing," she says. "When I went into labor, I called a cab, took myself to the hospital and had the baby."

"What about your family?" I ask. Surely she has someone to count on when she needs it.

She shrugs. "My parents divorced when I was little. I don't have much of a relationship with my dad and my mom is…well, she's always been more preoccupied with living her own life than participating in mine."

"What's Elan's last name?" I ask.

"Why?" she looks up to meet my eyes.

"I want to kick his fucking ass, that's why." My chest feels tight and my knuckles are itching to be busted over something – preferably his face.

"It's okay, Pace. I'm over Elan now. Completely. The only thing that still makes my heart hurt is knowing that one day I'll have to answer questions from Max about why his own father wanted nothing to do with him."

"I'm sorry I pried into all of this. I know it's none of my business." I feel like a grade-A asshole.

"It's okay," she says, digging her bare toes into the warm sand, her sandals long ago kicked aside. "It's taught me that I need to be better at picking men. A beautiful man with a smooth tongue who says all the right things doesn't excite me anymore."

She's letting me inside, and I appreciate the glimpse at her inner thoughts. Turning to face her, I ask, "What does excite you?"

"A man who is kind to my child."

Her answer is so poised, so simple; I can tell she means it entirely.

I wonder if that's how she views me. I hope so. I genuinely enjoyed playing with Max today and I hope she doesn't think I did it just to try and get into her panties. Which is what she probably expects, based on the stories she's heard from Colt. That shithead. My resolve to kick his ass is back again, full force.

"At the point I'm at, actions speak louder than words," she says. "I should probably go, I've said too much, I'm sure."

"Don't go. Not yet." I'm laying myself bare, so much more so than I ever do. My game is completely fucking shot, and I don't care.

"This isn't what my life is like, Pace. It's not all backyard barbecues where there are lots of helping hands, or fancy galas downtown."

"I get that, Kylie. You have responsibilities. I see that."

"It's hard work, Pace, and it's a twenty-four seven job. No sick days. No time off. And I know you'll say it doesn't matter – but it does. You're a Drake. I've seen the lives you guys lead. It's champagne and caviar and designer everything."

She has no way of knowing, but I'm not really like my brothers in that regard. I live in a simple two-bedroom condo, not a mansion on the beach like Colton and Collins each do. "A man gets tired of champagne and caviar after a while," I say, trying to make light of her jab.

"So you want to slum it for a while?"

"You are not slumming it. Max is not slumming it."

Her eyes flash on mine and I can tell that my words have touched something inside of her. "No, but we're not what you're used to."

"Maybe I'm tired of the same old–same old." I look her straight in the eyes as I say this, letting my meaning sink in.

She matches my serious gaze with one of her own. "And what about when you get tired of us? I can't have my son getting attached, only to have you disappear one day when you decide you're done playing house."

Damn. She's better at this verbal sparring than me, and I fucking hate it.

"I still want to take you to dinner," I say.

"I appreciate it, but I'm just not ready for anything like that." Kylie rises to her feet, and heads for the house. "Goodnight Pace."

Fuck.

We'd had a great night and just when we'd finally started to make some progress, she completely shot me down. I was tired of being told that I wasn't mature enough to handle the responsibility of dating a woman with a child. I wanted a fair chance. But as I watched her walk away, the defeated set to her shoulders, I realized she didn't *want* to be right about me. She just expected me to let her down.

"Kylie, wait up," I call, hopping to my feet and sprinting after her. I catch her on the patio where she's stuffing their things into a bag. Stray toys, a sippy cup and a baggie of cereal are all scattered at her feet. She lifts her chin and her eyes find mine. Confusion washes over her features. "Let me help you get Max to the car," I explain.

She doesn't respond. She just gazes up at me. But since she didn't refuse, I reach down and take the bag from her, adding the stray items and zipping it up. "I got this."

She watches me with mild curiosity, her pretty green eyes wide, like she's taking it all in, trying to dissect what I'm doing when she just shot me down a mere thirty seconds ago. Hell, I don't even know. I'm just following my instincts. I'm not trying to impress her or play some game, and it's incredibly refreshing.

Kylie's quiet as we head into the house. I'm not sure where Max is sleeping, but she leads me into the den. It's dark and silent, except for the little breathy sounds coming from the sleeping infant. He's on the floor on some type of sleeping mat. We stand over him for just a second, watching him. His mouth lifts in his sleep, and I suddenly find myself wondering what he could be dreaming about. Probably his pretty momma. A thought that warms me.

"May I?" I whisper.

She nods and takes the bag from me. I bend down and ever so gently lift the little guy from the floor. I bring him up to my chest, holding him close. He opens one eye, checking to see who's got him, and then drops his head to my shoulder, where it rests all the way to the car. His limp little body molds to mine, and I can feel his hot breath against my neck. Smiling, I give his back a gentle pat, careful not to wake him.

Kylie watches everything, then opens the door to the backseat and I place him in his car-seat while she leans over me and buckles him in. The scent of vanilla and delicate feminine skin wafts up to greet me. The scent awakens something in me. Perhaps it was watching her with her baby all afternoon, seeing her as a mother, and now experiencing the softness of her as a woman that stirs something in me. Compared to the one-dimensional women I usually date, it's a welcome reprieve.

Standing in the driveway with the moonlight pouring down on us, neither of us says a word. Kylie closes the car door and we both check through the window to see if the sound woke Max. It didn't.

"I could have gotten him," she says, turning to me.

"I know."

She watches me intently, as if trying to figure out my angle. It's the same look she gave me when I took Max from her earlier to show him the frog I had found in the garden.

"Drive safe," I tell her.

"I will." Without another word, she slips into the driver's seat.

I remain rooted in the driveway until she pulls away and I can no longer see her taillights. It hasn't even been two minutes, and I'm already plotting out ways to see her again.

Inside I find Sophie stationed at the kitchen island, her mouth stuffed full of a bite of cake.

I grin when I spot her and her eyes widen like she's been caught.

"Don't look at me like that," she says, licking the frosting from her thumb. "I barely got to eat with all the mingling and talking."

Holding up my hands, I motion for her to continue. "Don't stop on my account." I grab a slice of the cake with my fingers. "Here, I'll even join you. Cheers."

"Cheers." She touches the edge of her cake to mine and we eat in silence, enjoying the comfortable moment between us. Sophie already feels like family, so much more so than Colton's ex. That was one woman I couldn't stand being near. Sophie, I wouldn't mind cloning. That thought instantly makes me sad. She had a twin sister that she lost. I can still see a touch of sadness in her eyes, but considering everything, she's doing great.

We eat, moving on to the appetizer trays containing cheese puffs and crab rolls, while Sophie tells me stories of all the extended relatives and friends of the family she met tonight.

"I need your opinion on something," I say, wiping my hands on a cloth napkin.

"Wow, Pace needs me for something...I feel honored," she says, grinning at me. "What is it?"

"There's a woman I'm interested in," I start.

Footsteps behind me cause me to turn. It's Colton, looking for his bride-to-be, no doubt.

"As long as it's not Kylie, go to town," he says.

I hiss out a breath. "I like her, dude. What's your problem?" I'd intended to have a calm, rational conversation with Sophie. I already know my brother's views on this, and it pisses me off.

"She's a single mom," Colton says, like I don't know this fact.

"I'm well aware. Do you think I missed the mini-human who was attached to her hip all night?" I actually viewed him as a sort of bonus.

Sophie's watching all of this, her eyes whipping back and forth between us as she struggles to catch up. "Maybe it wouldn't be so bad, Colton," she says, placing her hand on his arm. "Pace is a nice guy. Kylie's a sweet girl."

Colton laughs out loud. *The fucker.* "Pace is not a nice guy."

Sophie's eyes fly to mine again, and her lips purse out as if she's weighing this information.

"The only reason I'm not going to kill you is because it would upset Sophie," I bit out, glaring at him.

"He's sweet, Colton," she says, as if trying to convince us both. Her innocence is adorable.

"He's nice to you, sweetness, because he knows I'd kill him otherwise," Colton tells her, planting a kiss on her neck.

"Pace?" she asks.

"Don't listen to him, cupcake. I can be nice. I'll be the first to admit, a lot of the girls I've gone out with in the past have been...temporary playthings."

Sophie's eyebrows dart up.

I shrug. "I'm just speaking the truth. But I understand the difference between that and a quality girl like Kylie."

"Colt, will you give us a minute, darling? I just want to talk to Pace," Sophie says.

He presses his lips to hers, and grunts out a reply. Reluctantly dragging his mouth away from hers, he finally leaves us alone.

Sophie turns back to me, her expression serious. "So you like her?" she asks.

"I do." There's just something about her. Maybe I'm starting to outgrow the sloppy drunken hookups that my weekends usually consist of. Maybe I'm ready for something real.

"So what's the problem? I know you won't let Colton's opinion stand in your way."

"Nah. He'll get over it. I wanted your advice because Kylie doesn't seem interested in me. Which is something quite new for me." I grin crookedly and shrug. I sound like a cocky asshole, but it's the truth.

"My advice? Honestly? Go get her, tiger." She gives me a playful smirk.

"With all due respect, what the hell do you mean, cupcake?"

"I'm going to let you in on a secret." She pats the stool beside her, indicating I should sit. I do. "A girl likes it when her man goes all alpha male on her ass," she continues.

"What are you saying?"

"Like when Colton refused to accept that I had left. He flew to Italy to win me back."

I remember that trip well. I'd actually tried to talk him out of it. It's great to woo the girl you love, but he was married at the time. I told him he should deal with his baggage first, but his plan had worked. "You're saying I shouldn't take no for an answer?"

"Exactly. Go win her over. Show her why you two would be great together."

How the hell do I do that? I rub my temples. I picture her and her baby son. An idea takes hold, and refuses to let go.

"I got this, Soph."

She grins at me adoringly. "I always knew you did."

Chapter Five

KYLIE

Today has been exhausting, and it's only noon. With Max's nanny out of town for the next two weeks for a long overdue honeymoon, I know I'm going to have my hands full. We've played trucks, kicked balls around the yard, finger-painted on sheets of construction paper, made up songs, danced, read books and now I'm ready for a nap. Of course Max is still raring to go.

With Max content for a moment to explore the little plastic farm I've set down in front of him, I plop down onto the couch and kick my feet up onto the oversized ottoman.

I can't help my mind drifting back to yesterday and how it felt to see Pace with my son. If there was ever a form of foreplay for a single mom – watching an attractive, attentive man interact with your child was it. Max is my heart, and so observing how careful and sweet Pace was with him made me feel all kinds of things I'd rather not admit.

A knock at the door breaks my little daydream and Max's head pops up. I push myself up off the couch, wondering who it could be as Max races toward it. I need to teach him about stranger danger.

I pull open the door and am momentarily stunned into silence.

It's Pace.

He's standing on my front porch holding an inflated baby pool and a bagful of water toys.

What in the hell?

He's dressed in a simple white t-shirt and dark jeans that hint at the muscle beneath, and a pair of leather flip flops on his long tan feet. His eyes dart from mine down to the baby at my feet and a slow smile overtakes his mouth.

"Hope you don't mind…Sophie mentioned that your nanny is going to be out of town for the next few weeks…I thought maybe you guys could use some company…"

"I…uh…" I'm at a loss for words apparently. Men don't show up at my house with toys. Especially not men this utterly attractive that make my breasts perk up, my nipples pushing against the lace of my bra, demanding attention. *Son of bitch!*

Pace's eyes wander from mine downward and I cross my arms over my chest. That damn dimple adorns his cheek while his mouth curls into a crooked grin.

Pace's gaze continues down until he reaches Max, who's currently hiding behind my legs.

"Hey little man," Pace says.

All I can think about is the fact that there's a gorgeous man on my porch and I'm unshowered, unshaven, dressed in a tank top that shows my ratty old bra straps and, oh dear God….a pair of maternity shorts I hung onto because they were sooo comfortable. My child is thirteen months old and I'm still in maternity clothes. What is wrong with me? I've lost the baby weight – all except for the last ten pounds and the muffin top that sits at my waistband. I vow here and now to begin a gym regimen soon. Tomorrow. And to throw these damn maternity shorts away. In the three seconds I've taken to ponder all of this, Max has emerged from behind my legs and charges straight at Pace.

He slams into Pace, full force, hitting him straight between the legs.

"Omph," Pace releases a strangled grunt and doubles over, dropping the toys to cup his battered manhood.

"Oh God, are you alright?" I spring into action, removing Max from around Pace's leg.

"Just give me a minute," he bites out.

I feel terrible, but then I decide that's crazy. He's the one who showed up unannounced and uninvited, and Max didn't intentionally hurt him.

Max, oblivious to the pain he's just caused, climbs into the pool that is now lying on the porch.

Composing himself after several moments, Pace stands, rising to his full height. "Strong little guy," he comments.

He really is. We wrestle every night, and he wins. "Pace?" I ask, still wondering what on earth he's doing at my house.

"It's a beautiful day." He smiles, looking straight up at the cloudless blue sky. "Care for a swim?"

Since Max is already in the pool, I know I can't refuse. "Sure. Do you want to take that around back? I'll get Max changed and we'll meet you out there."

He grins at me, knowing he's won this round. Sneaky. I just wish I knew what he was up to.

When I lift Max from the pool, he kicks and screams, until I explain that he needs to put his bathing suit on, and then he relents, letting me tow him back inside the house.

Through Max's bedroom window, I can see Pace setting up the pool, and dragging my garden hose over to fill it.

I quickly strip Max down and get him into a swim diaper and his red swimming trunks. Then I grab the baby sunblock and my sunglasses, and we join Pace in the backyard.

Max toddles toward him without hesitation. *Be careful, baby, this man could hurt us.*

Pace has dumped the bag of water toys into the filling pool – the colorful balls, buckets and floating plastic animals capture Max's attention and he lets out a loud squeal and begins clapping his hands. He doesn't have a swimming pool, but given how much he loves bath time, I know he's going to love this.

As he gets near the water, I reach out for Max.

"I've got him," Pace says, closing two big hands around Max's tummy and lifting him into the water so that he can dip his feet.

Max kicks his feet and giggles, clearly enjoying himself.

I feel wary and on edge. I know I said too much last night, and I don't know what Pace must think of me now.

Max sits down in the pool, and I turn off the hose – three inches of water is enough for him to splash around in.

I sit down in the grass beside Pace, both of us watching Max. At least with him capturing our attention, the pressure is off to make small talk. Yet as the minutes pass, I can't seem to relax in the presence of this big, beautiful man who came baring gifts and is playing with my son.

"Pace, I don't mean to sound ungrateful, because it's very sweet of you to bring Max a pool and toys, but I need to understand what this is." I'm thankful for the cover of my dark sunglasses because his gaze settles squarely on mine and his look is serious and intense.

"I get that this is a big deal, and it's scary. It's not just you. You've got this little guy to look out for." He pats the top of Max's head, ruffling his hair. "And you don't know my intentions."

I nod. That's it exactly. He knows about how Max's dad abandoned us. I eagerly await his answer, practically holding my breath.

Pace meets my eyes, his deep blue gaze cutting straight into mine. "So I'll make this crystal clear: I like you, Kylie. I like Max. I came here today because I enjoyed spending time with you and I wanted to see you again."

"Pace, I'm sorry, it's just that after Max's dad, I'm really not looking for anything." The idea of casually dating terrifies me.

"If you never try, how you will know?"

He's right. I know he is, but the logical part of my brain tells me to be careful. The next man I date needs to be husband material. And I'm nowhere near ready for that anyhow. Judging by Pace's good looks and carefree lifestyle, I'm sure he enjoys no-strings sex, nightclubs, and women without stretch marks. But then again, I'd thought Elan was husband material. He'd been mature and settled, and look how well that had turned out for me.

Pace is smooth, but not overtly so. There's a truth in his eyes when he speaks the words. My brain is just hyper aware of men who promise me nice things and push me to want more.

Max slips against the bottom of the pool, sliding under and comes up sputtering from the mouthful of water he's swallowed. Before I can even react, Pace has scooped him up and is holding Max to his chest, patting his back to clear his airway and murmuring encouragingly

My hands are shaking, but Max is fine. Thank God.

I grab Max's beach towel and wrap him up, clinging to him and kissing his head.

"He's alright, Kylie. I had him," Pace says, his tone defeated.

"I know." I look over at Pace and see that his t-shirt is soaked and is clinging to his tanned skin. My belly tightens and a warm tingly sensation spreads through me. Geez, it's been way too long. "Do you want to come inside and get dried off?" My voice comes out strained and I inhale deeply, trying to regain my composure. "I can make us lunch," I offer.

Pace nods and fishes all the water toys from the pool, setting them aside so they can dry, then he follows me and Max inside.

I know we didn't finish our conversation from earlier, the one where he challenged me to take a chance and live a little, which is good – because I have no response. "I'll be just a minute, make yourself comfortable," I tell him.

I get Max changed into a dry diaper and a new outfit – his favorite blue t-shirt with an alligator on the front and a pair of shorts. And since I'm now wet too, I take the opportunity to change into something more appropriate for having company over. A sleeveless midnight blue dress. It's cotton and stretchy and soft, and I hope doesn't give off the impression I'm trying too hard. I finger-comb my tangled hair and pull it back into a low ponytail.

When Max and I emerge from the bedrooms, I find Pace standing in my living room, looking at the photographs of Max that I have on pretty much every surface with a wistful expression on his face.

He's stripped off his wet t-shirt and when he turns to face me, I feel like someone has punched me in the stomach. All of the air has been sucked from my lungs.

His chest and abs are rock solid muscle, like they've been carved from stone. He's tan and has a light spattering of dark hair that disappears under the waistband of his jeans...and speaking of waistbands, there are no boxers or briefs that I can see. Does he go commando? And why do my fingers itch to find out?

"Do you have a dryer?" he asks, holding up a damp t-shirt.

"Y-yes," I stammer and point to the hall that leads to the laundry room. A shirtless Pace and I'm reduced to one word answers and pointing. Excellent.

His gaze wanders over my curves, stopping at the knee-length hemline of my dress and he smiles appreciatively. "Be right back."

I hear the dryer start up and I head into the kitchen, securing Max in his highchair and begin removing ingredients from the fridge.

"I'm sorry I can't offer you anything more sophisticated than grilled cheese sandwiches," I tell him.

"I haven't had a grilled cheese in years. Sounds great." Pace beams at me.

Why is he always so sure and steady when I feel anything but?

Pace plays with Max while I busy myself buttering slices of bread and tucking cheese between them. It takes every ounce of willpower I have not to turn around and watch them interact – the sweet sounds of baby babbling, coupled with deep male laughter tug at my heartstrings. *Don't be fooled by this pretty man, Kylie.*

When the sandwiches are ready, I cut Max's into little bites and dump the whole thing on his tray. Then I toss in some raspberries and his cup of milk. Pace watches me move around my kitchen and the sign language I use to communicate with Max. If he wants to hang around, he's going to have to get used to the pecking order here. Max's needs come first.

When I finally set our plates down at the kitchen island where Pace is sitting, I'm expecting him to make some comment about how the sandwiches are now cold, but instead he turns to me and smiles.

"You're a really good mom."

No one's ever said that to me before and the emotional impact of his words stop me dead in my tracks. It's as though all of my edge that I've fought to keep – my strength, determination and the lady balls I've had to grow since becoming a single mom – all of it is wiped out in an instant. "T-thank you," I murmur.

Pace takes a bite of the sandwich, his eyes not straying from Max. "What's that sign mean?" he asks.

I look over at Max and see his little fingers opening and closing. "Milk," I say.

"I've got it." Pace stands, and grabs the empty cup from his tray.

My feelings toward him soften, as I watch him pour milk into the sippy cup, fasten the lid tightly and place it back in Max's chubby grasp.

I don't need any help, but damn his presence here feels good. So good. I'm tired of being strong all the time. Here is a man, a gorgeous fucking man, who is willing to help.

Why not let him? The lump in my throat makes it difficult to swallow.

PACE

I'm amazed to be here, sharing this moment with Kylie and her son. It's something so normal – having lunch – yet it feels like so much more. Her eyes stay glued to me as I move around the kitchen, helping clean off Max's hands and dumping the remnants of his tray of food into the trash.

After lunch, Kylie lays Max down in his crib for a nap, and then rejoins me in the living room. She begins picking up toys and tossing them into a basket beside the couch. I get the sense she doesn't often have downtime – time just for herself – time to be a woman and not just a mom. It's strange how being near her makes me think of things I've never before considered.

"Come sit down for a bit," I encourage, patting the seat next to me.

She does, falling back into the plush sofa with a soft sigh. "I love him, but God, he's exhausting," she laughs.

"He's great," I say.

Her eyes slide over to mine and she studies me quietly, her face suddenly serious.

Today hasn't been about romance. We weren't trying to impress one another, well, maybe I was trying a little – showing up here with that pool, but I wonder if all of this – the slow start, the conversation, the getting to know someone, is the key to it all. Talking, building a friendship first, having it lead to something on a deeper level than I've ever operated at before. I've never approached a relationship with a woman like this before. And it feels so entirely different, I'm beside myself for what comes next.

It's been interesting seeing her in her space all day. Unlike my tidy and sparse condo, her house actually feels like a home. It feels lived in and alive. There are candid photographs on the walls and decorating the shelves and mantle. Selfies with her and Max, or just Max alone, because she's the one behind the camera. There are no happy family portraits, just a beautiful girl who doesn't understand her worth, and her baby son.

"So what's a swinging single man like you doing on a play date on a Saturday?" she asks.

"Swinging, huh?" I lift an eyebrow, watching her.

"Swinging."

"You have heard the stories, huh?"

"Sure have."

"I'm going to kill Colton," I say.

"I figured, but seriously, nothing better to do today than play with a one year old?"

"You know why I'm here, Kylie." At least she should.

"Enlighten me."

"The playdate with Max was a rouse. I'm actually kind of digging his mom."

She laughs, her eyes not straying from mine.

"That wasn't obvious? I figured I had no game and you were on to me."

"Is that what all this is to you? A game?" she asks, her voice suddenly going serious.

"Of course not." This is the most real experience I've had in a long time.

"You make me nervous, Pace. You make me want things I didn't think I could have."

"Same here," I answer.

"Explain."

"Being here today, this is all new for me. I'm just as much out of my element as you are."

"I doubt that," she challenges, her voice steady.

"Hanging out with a woman and her child? It's something I've never done, never wanted to do before…but you make me want to try something new. I'll be the first to admit, sex is all I know. It's been my way of life for the past…" I do a quick mental calculation… "Twelve years." From seducing my high school chemistry teacher to fucking the housekeeper, to sleeping my way through the LA singles scene for the fun of it. It was the only thing I was good at. I've always been the fun one – the guy you called for a good time. Yet now, in the face of this gorgeous woman, it all seemed fucking pointless. Had I even derived any pleasure from it? "Maybe I'm getting tired of the same-old, same-old," I tell her. I pause, watching her reaction. Kylie is closely watching me, breathing softly through parted lips, but she's quiet and still.

"I can't take a chance on maybes and somedays. I have too much at stake, too much to lose to gamble like that."

"If you were any other woman, I'd be balls deep inside of you by now. Trust me, I can be different, you make me feel different."

Her cheeks flush pink and her pulse thrums at the side of her neck.

"Does that make you nervous?"

She nods. "Y-yes."

"Why?" I don't know if we're talking about the sex, or the fact that I want to stick around.

"There's been no one since Elan," she says.

She's been with no one since…nine months of pregnancy and now Max is thirteen months old… Nearly two years. Damn. That's a long ass time to be celibate. Way too long.

"Don't you miss it?" I ask.

"It? Meaning cock?" Her mouth lifts in a sassy grin.

"Among other things. Intimacy is what I was referring to."

"And what does a man like you know of intimacy?"

She hasn't answered my question, yet hers is spot on, stripping me bare, making me look inside at the man I am and examining him in the harsh light. There is nothing intimate about a quick fuck in a bathroom stall at a nightclub with a girl whose name and face I won't remember in the morning. Even if I don't like examining my past in her presence, I love her ability to challenge me.

"I know that I haven't spent this much time talking, getting to know a woman in a long, long time," I say.

I lift her hand from where it rests on the couch between us. I know we both feel this pull —this tug of sexual awareness and energy and desire. It permeates the air around us, drawing me to her.

"Tell me what you need," I ask, lacing my fingers with her. The simple act of holding her hand makes my blood pump faster.

Her eyes land hesitantly on mine. They are full of questions. "I need you to be careful. With me and with Max," she whispers.

"Done."

Her eyes study mine, like she's looking for clues that she can trust me.

"I don't say things I don't mean, Kylie. I never have. I don't promise things I can't give."

She nods, imperceptibly. "I still don't understand... I've seen the women you're attracted to. You like them blonde, busty and compliant. Not short, sassy and with ten extra pounds of baby weight."

"You want to know what I see when I look at you?"

I release her hand to cup her cheek. She inhales sharply at the sudden contact. She continues watching me, waiting to see what I'll say next.

"I see strength, and softness combined in the most exquisite package. I see a mother who loves her child with every ounce of her being. But I don't see just a mother. I also see a *woman*, a stunningly beautiful woman with a lush body, and full, heavy breasts, and lips that I very much want to kiss."

I hold her eyes, letting my words sink in while my thumb makes slow circles against her cheek.

Her eyes flutter on mine and her breath becomes shallow. She's waiting for me to kiss her, but I won't rush this. I let the moment sink in–let her feel–truly feel every bit of the lust building between us, because by her own admission, this feeling is something she's denied herself for too long.

Unconsciously she leans closer and my hand slides from her cheek around to the back of her neck. I guide her mouth to mine and watch her eyes slip closed just before our mouths meet. Her lips are soft and full and easily mold to mine, letting me lead the kiss.

She is so stunning, my dick is already hard.

I kiss her gently at first, letting her adjust to the sensations, then suck her lower lip into my mouth, tugging her closer. I need more.

Kylie lets out a soft groan and the throb in my pants intensifies as my cock presses uncomfortably against my zipper.

Christ, I've never been this hard from a kiss alone. At least not since the ninth grade, when I was plotting out how to get my hand into the front of Rachel Lundquist's jeans while we made out.

Using both hands, I hold Kylie's face as I kiss her deeply, loving the feel of her tongue thrusting against mine. She denies me nothing, her mouth freely moves against mine and tiny moans vibrate in her throat.

Kylie's hands begin wandering along my chest and abs and I begin praying to any gods who will listen that she continues her path south. I know her son is in the next room, and I know that's not what today is about, but I'm dying to feel her delicate hands wrapped around my cock.

Rubbing her hands along my chest, Kylie steals my breath. She gingerly touches my abs, her small hands sliding over the grooves as she explores. Her touch is much more innocent than I'm used to, yet it feels fucking incredible and so erotic, because I know how big of a deal this is for her. But what she does next totally surprises me.

Kylie climbs into my lap, straddling me, and aligns her core so she's pressed against my erection.

Christ.

She's warm and sitting right against my cock.

I want to show her there's not a goddamn thing wrong with her body, and I bring my hands to her ass and thrust up so she can feel how much I want her.

Kylie whimpers and grips my biceps as she rubs herself against me. Her tongue is stroking mine and I imagine what her hot mouth would feel like around the head of my cock, what her tongue would feel like licking along my swollen shaft and almost come in my pants.

Shit, her curvy body working against mine is a magical thing.

When I arrived here today, my goal was only to get her to trust me – now my goal is to make her come. I want to hear her moan out my name and know that I'm the man taking care of her.

I'd never gone this slow with a woman, but suddenly I'm starting to see the merits in taking my time, in letting her get comfortable and control the pace.

I can't resist bringing my hands to her breasts. They are soft and lush and most definitely fucking real. When my thumbs graze her nipples, she chokes on a groan.

"Pace…What are we doing?" she asks, her voice breathless and husky. Her hips still against mine.

No, no, no. Don't question it.

"Shh…Don't think. Just come," I tell her. I pluck her nipples through the thin cotton dress she's wearing and feel them harden. Kylie whimpers and buries her face against my neck. Her hips thrust up and down against me.

Yes, that's it.

Despite us both being clothed, her movements mimic her riding my dick and I feel like I'm about to explode.

I love the way her breasts fit perfectly in my hands, and the breathy cries she makes when I graze her nipples. If she doesn't get off soon, I'm going to come in my pants, which would not be cool.

I kiss the side of her neck, the dip in her throat. "Does that feel good?" I ask.

"Yes," she breathes. "Oh God, Pace. I think I'm going to…"

"Fuck yeah. That's it, angel."

She's found her rhythm and bounces against me, grinding her hips as she lifts and lowers. I bite down on my cheek, cursing out my cock. The bastard better behave and not embarrass me.

I caress her nipples through the fabric of her dress and bra, wishing it was my tongue teasing them rather than my fingers. I want to taste her pussy, and watch her come undone, I want to thrust inside her slow and deep until she gasps. I want so much more with her, but

I will settle for this moment–because I know this is huge.

"Pace...Pace..." she breathes out, pushing her fingers into my hair.

"That's right. Come for me." I give her nipples a tug and Kylie comes apart, trembling as the orgasm hits her.

She breathes out my name a final time and we kiss until she stops spasming.

We sit like that together, her in my lap, our heartbeats pounding together, and nothing has ever felt more right.

After a moment, she scrambles off my lap and buries her face in her hands. "Oh my God, I can't believe I just did that. I'm sorry. I don't know what came over me. I haven't had attention from a man in such a long time, I just..."

I press a finger over her lips quieting her. "Stop. First of all, that was the hottest fucking thing I've ever seen." Her getting herself off by humping my dick? Yeah, that was better than any porn video. "And second, I like that you haven't been with a man in a while. I like that you're cautious. You're smart.

And you're beautiful. You're the total package."

"Yeah…some package." She rolls her eyes and I notice that her cheeks are still pink from her orgasm. "I just dry-humped you and oh God, this is just so embarrassing."

"Don't do that," I warn, my tone firm. "You're incredibly sexy and if what you've said is true—that you haven't gotten off with a man in what, two years? Then I feel incredibly fucking honored."

She blushes again. "Yeah, crazy, huh?" Her shoulders straighten, and she looks slightly more put together. "And how long has been it been since you've gotten off with a woman?"

I consider it for a moment. "Tuesday?" It was the day before I went to Colton's office to ask about Kylie. It had been my attempt to push her out of my brain. I'd taken the towel attendant at my new gym back into the locker room and fucked her. It would be the first and last time I attended that center.

Kylie's look is pure disgust. She smacks me in the face with a toss pillow. "You pig."

"I told you I'd always be honest with you."

Her look softens. "Yes, that's true. Actually, I appreciate that."

"Good. And seriously, you have nothing to be embarrassed about. You're smoking hot—I almost fucking came in my pants watching you."

Her eyes drift down, and I know she can see I'm still hard. Yeah, I'll be dealing with the beast later. He behaved himself today and deserves to be rewarded. But I'll worry about that later. Kylie's son is here, and the first time we're together, I'll make sure we have complete privacy.

"How long does the little guy sleep?" I ask.

"Usually an hour or two."

"Nice." I kick my feet up on the ottoman in front of the couch and lean back, tugging Kylie against me. She curls into my side and exhales softly.

We sit in comfortable silence for several minutes, and thankfully the erection from hell fades.

"Max had a blast with you today. What are you doing next weekend?" She laughs uneasily.

Little does she know I'd happily repeat this entire day. Then I remember the plans I'd tentatively made with some college buddies.

"I might check out a music festival down in San Diego with some friends. Borrow Colton's jet while he's away. You should come," I say.

Kylie stiffens and then pulls away from me. When I meet her eyes, they are filled with sadness and distrust.

What the hell?

KYLIE

It's been an amazing afternoon with Pace. I'd let my guard down completely. And with one little innocuous statement, my bubble is burst. I can't just jet off for the weekend. He and I lead very different lives. And this time around, I won't ignore the warning signs and try to make us into something we can never be. I'd be a fool to believe that weekends at home with a crying baby and cold grilled cheese sandwiches would be enough for a man like Pace. I'd made that mistake once with Max's father—put my heart on the line—only to have it crushed when he left. I can't go through that again. Won't.

Pace is looking at me like he's confused. He has no idea what changed between us in the span of ten minutes—in between me grinding up and down against his rather impressive erection, and then me being forced back into the reality of our very different lives.

"Kylie?" He sits up straight and reaches for me.

I shake my head. I won't explain my sudden change of heart to him, because he'll only try to rationalize it away. He'll say it doesn't matter, that he doesn't mind canceling his weekend plans, and then three years from now, he'll resent me for trying to control him. I like my life—I'm fine with my simple weekends at home with Max, but I know that won't be enough for a man like Pace. He looks like he fell out of the pages of a J. Crew catalog—he's effortlessly sexy and cool, and of course he's flying a bunch of friends in a private jet to catch some band I've never even heard of. It'll always be that way. There's just too much distance between us. His family is insanely wealthy and are used to getting whatever they want. I'll be celebrating my thirtieth birthday this year, and he's just twenty-five, with a perfectly fit body, six-pack abs and a gleaming, white smile. He and I come from different worlds. And while it's sweet of him to try, and I feel incredibly flattered by his attention, I know it'd never work in the long run. Best to put a stop to it now.

"I think it's time for you to go, Pace." I rise to my feet, and I watch as his expression hardens. As much as it hurts my heart to walk away now, it'd be a thousand times worse once Max and I are attached.

He reaches out for me, cupping his palm on my cheek. "Hang on a second. What happened there?"

Damn. I draw in a deep, steadying breath. He's not going to drop it until I explain myself. "You're nice, and you're sweet to come here and hang out with us today, but I think we both know this would never work out anyhow."

"I don't know that." His thumb skitters back and forth slowly across my skin and little tingles of pleasure from the simple touch remind me how very long it's been since I've been so tenderly touched. *Focus, Kylie.*

I say the one and only thing I know he cannot argue with. "I'm just not ready."

He rises to his feet and watches me. The pulse in his neck is jumping, and his hands are clenched into tight fists. He looks like he wants to argue with me, but something stops him.

"It was sweet of you to come over and bring Max a gift today, but this isn't going anywhere."

Pace looks dejected. He reaches into his pocket and places a business card in my hand. "If you need anything while Colton and Sophie are out of town, call me."

I nod.

Pace leaves and since Max is still asleep, I head to my room and fall heavily onto the bed, curl into a ball, and cry.

I cry for my lonely heart, I cry for my fatherless son, I cry because I just kicked a beautiful, thoughtful man out of my house, and I hate myself for it. I wish that he would have fought for me. But why would he? With each encounter we've had, I've ended it by telling him that we'd never work. He was bound to start believing me sooner or later, and maybe this time it stuck.

When I go out on a date again, it'll be with someone who's looking for a serious commitment. I've been down the seemingly reformed player road before, and we all know how that turned out. And Elan's manwhore-like past had been much further behind him than Pace's. But when I found out I was pregnant, he left. He left me and the little body growing inside me without so much as a backward glance.

I live with absolutely no regrets though. I can't imagine life without Max. He keeps me steady. He grounds me. Just knowing there's someone who relies on me for literally everything—his food, safety, and comfort, it's humbling. And the moment I laid eyes upon him after twenty hours of labor, I made him a promise that I would never let him down.

I wipe away my foolish tears and close my eyes. I'm so tired. Exhausted actually. Being strong all the time is tiring. My body feels heavy against the mattress, and my breathing slows. Just as I feel myself falling under, Max begins to cry.

I climb from bed, forcing on a smile as I prepare to do it all over again.

Here we go.

PACE

The blonde bobbing up and down on my cock is slobbering too much. Her noises are too fake, her hair is too platinum, but mostly she's not Kylie.

It's been a week since I've seen her. A week since I've heard that sweet baby giggle, and watched them interact as mother and son. My erection threatens to fade, and I thread my fingers in her hair, pushing her head up and down. The satisfaction I get from her mouth is minimal, but it's better than my own hand on my dick, which has been a nightly occurrence since I'd watched Kylie get herself off by rubbing against me.

"Take me deep," I growl.

Blondie's moans increase in volume, but thankfully, so does her suction.

"Don't stop," I tell her, keeping one hand on the back of her head to show her how I need it.

When I picture Kylie's careful composure crumbling as she took her pleasure from me, a fresh surge of blood pumps south, making me fully hard again. I remember her whimpers and how full and soft her breasts felt in my hands, and I come with a roar, burying my hands in Blondie's hair as I release in her mouth.

The orgasm doesn't even come close to satisfying the feelings of discontent stewing inside me. I've never been flat out rejected by a woman. At least not until Kylie. Turns out I don't like it. Not one bit.

I tuck my flaccid dick back into my pants and zip up. Blondie is watching me expectantly. Knowing that I won't see her again, I don't care that she hadn't gotten off. I know that makes me an asshole, but I don't care.

Just as I'm looking for the words to get her out of my office, my cell phone starts ringing. I fish it from my pocket, thankful for the distraction from Blondie's watery blue eyes. A number I don't recognize flashes on the screen and normally I'd let it go to voicemail, but something tells me I need to pick it up.

"Hello?"

"Pace? It's Kylie. I need you." Her voice is weak, and she sounds scared.

My stomach tightens, and my heart begins pounding. "Where are you?"

"At the emergency room."

"What happened? Is Max okay?" My tone is almost frantic and a sour feeling pooling in the pit of my stomach.

"He's fine. It's actually me… I took a bad fall. Can you come get me?"

"Of course. I'll be there in fifteen minutes."

"Thank you."

Blondie's frown tells me she's not happy about the half of the conversation she overheard. Too fucking bad. Kylie needs me, and I will be there for her.

***

I take Max from one of the emergency room nurses and follow her into in Kylie's hospital room. She's sitting on the bed, holding her arm awkwardly in her lap. My heart clenches at the sight of her. This normally strong, resilient woman looks pale, exhausted, and tiny sitting in the hospital bed.

"Hey." I bend down and kiss her cheek. It's such a natural response that I don't realize until after my lips are on her skin that it's probably not appropriate. Oh-fucking-well.

"Thank you for coming. Max was getting out of hand. They have to fit me for a cast, and since they gave me some pain killers, they won't let me drive home." She reaches her good hand toward us and gives Max's foot a playful tug, trying to lighten the heaviness all around us.

"What happened?" I ask.

"I was working in the office above my garage and when I heard Max cry on the monitor, I went jogging downstairs to get him, and I slipped. I tumbled down the last half-dozen or so stairs. X-rays confirmed my arm is broken in two spots."

Shit. That's not good. The urge to pull her into my arms and kiss her is nearly overwhelming. Instead, I give Max a gentle squeeze. I get the sense that he's a buffer for each of us.

He lunges toward Kylie. "You've got to be gentle with your momma," I tell him, letting him sit beside her on the bed, where he promptly crawls into her lap. Kylie moves her broken arm to the side away from Max and winces in pain.

"Miss Sloan?" A nurse pokes her head into the room. "I'm ready to take you to get your cast now."

"Okay," Kylie says, then turns to me. "Will you take him to the cafeteria to get something to eat? I shouldn't be too long."

"Absolutely. Want to get some lunch, buddy?" I ask, lifting him into my arms.

Max looks to Kylie, who makes the sign for *eat*, then he lets out a squeal.

Okay then. It's settled. I have a lunch date with the world's cutest one-year-old.

"Good luck," I say to Kylie as the nurse leads her from the room. I can't help the worry that churns in my gut.

Later, on the drive home, I'm trying to think of a way to explain to Kylie that it's not a good idea for her to stay alone right now. But I know it will be a tricky subject. She barely let me strap him into his car seat. We'd moved it from her car into mine and left her car in the hospital parking lot.

"I still can't believe you drove yourself," I tell her.

She shrugs. "I didn't know it was actually broken. I didn't want to call an ambulance for nothing. It could have been a minor sprain."

"An arm broken in two spots is not nothing." Plus it's her right arm—her dominant hand—meaning life is going to be difficult for her for the next six weeks. I can see her beginning to process all of this when we pull into her driveway.

First I help her from the car, then I get Max, and carry him, along with her purse, to the front door. Fishing around inside her purse for her keys, I see baby toys and tampons and tubes of lipstick, but no keys. Finally she directs me to look in the outside pocket, and I let us all into the house.

"Thank you," she says, taking Max one-armed from me. "I'm sorry I interrupted your day. I hope you weren't busy when I called."

I remember that my cock had been in another woman's mouth moments before she called, and I feel like the world's biggest asshole. "No, I wasn't busy."

"Still, I feel bad. The last time we hung out..."

"I gave you my card and told you to call if you needed anything. I'm glad I was here today to help."

She nods. "Thank you for that. I didn't have anyone else to call. With my nanny still away on her honeymoon and Colton and Sophie in Africa ... it's going to be a tough week."

"It doesn't have to be," I say, gathering my courage for what I'm sure is about to lead to an argument.

"What do you mean?"

"Come stay with me."

"What? Me and Max? No. That's crazy."

"Kylie." I look straight into her eyes. "You couldn't even get him in and out of the car seat without help. How do you think it's going to go when you're alone and trying to fix him dinner, or give him a bath, or change his diaper, or do any of the other millions of things you do with him every day?"

"I'll manage, Pace. It's not your responsibility."

"Maybe I want it to be."

She watches me curiously, her eyes bouncing from mine, to Max, to the floor. "You want to change diapers?"

I shrug. "I want to help you. I couldn't sleep at night with the thought of you here, alone, injured and trying to be strong. I know you're strong. I know you can handle just about anything, but you don't have to do it alone. Let me help."

"The only reason I couldn't get him into the car seat today was because I'm still sore."

They'd given her some powerful painkillers, but I could tell she was still hurting. "And you're going to be sore for the next several days. You broke your arm, angel. Come on, let's pack a bag for you and for Max, and I'll show you my place. If you don't like it, or don't think it will work, I'll bring you guys right back here. Sound fair?"

She huffs out a deep breath. "I guess so. I don't even know where you live."

"I have a condo on the coast. You'll like it, I think." I treat her to a dimpled grin, and she rolls her eyes.

"Come on, Max." She leads us all back to the bedrooms where she tosses clothes and toys onto the bed, and I stuff them into a bag.

Chapter Six

When we arrive at my condo, I open the door and watch Kylie's reaction as she takes in the space. I certainly don't live in a mansion by any stretch of the imagination, but I like my place. I bought it two years ago when my business started taking off and got a great deal on it. I might have a trust fund like my brothers, but I make it a point not to live off the money. I like knowing that everything here—from the Persian wool rug on the cherry wood floors, to the dark gray sofa, to the oil paintings on the walls—I have bought and paid for with money I have earned.

It's an open floor plan, so pretty much everything except the bedrooms is visible. Kylie's eyes bounce from the living room to the kitchen, outfitted in stainless steel and granite. "Nice place," she comments, her voice small. It's a far cry from her cozy home with its throw pillows and oversized chairs and candid pictures on every available surface. My home lacks the personal touches hers has. I have only two photographs sitting on a shelf, collecting dust. One is of me and my brothers, taken two years ago during a yachting trip, and the other is my group of college buddies. James has a black eye in the photo, and Kylie leans close, looking at the picture.

"What happened to him?" she asks.

"Ah, it was his birthday," I say, not giving a further explanation of our drunken shenanigans. It was a long ass time ago.

"Do you go out and get rowdy like that often?" she asks, frowning.

"Not really." Not anymore. When you have to get up for work early the next day, the appeal of the late-night party scene fades considerably.

When Kylie sets Max down, he immediately toddles over to the floor-to-ceiling glass windows that have an ocean view, and begins slapping the glass.

"Come on, Max." She steers him away from the windows. "Wow, what a view," Kylie says, holding Max at her hip and admiring the blue water below.

"I like it." I grin, watching her. I like having her here, at my place. Already, there's new life breathed into the quiet space.

She lets Max explore while I show her around and in the span of fifteen minutes, he's riffled through my kitchen cabinets, and removed various dangerous looking kitchen apparatuses, crawled into the bathroom and stuck his hands in the toilet water, and now he's digging through the soil of a potted palm in my dining room. Kylie hasn't been able to relax for even a second, chasing him from room to room. This is not going well.

When I see my place through her eyes, I realize it's not nearly as baby-friendly as I thought. *Shit.* I want her to be comfortable here, but if she has to constantly worry about her son, she's not going to be. And she needs to heal.

"What about the sleeping arrangements?" she asks.

Shit. This is where things are going to go from bad to worse. I hadn't shown her the bedrooms yet, and for good reason. It's a two-bedroom condo, but one has been converted into an office.

"Come on," I say, grabbing her and Max's bags from near the front door. "This way."

I lead them down the back hallway, past the guest bath and toward my room. I know I hadn't made my bed that morning, but it was too late now. Hopefully I didn't leave any dirty clothes on the floor.

"This is the office," I point to the spare bedroom that holds a basic desk, laptop and chair. Nothing too exciting. "And this is my room." I enter through the double doorway, and she follows me inside. Her confusion is visible in her tense shoulders and squinty eyes that dart around the room. Max begins exploring while Kylie turns to face me. "W-where are we going to sleep?"

"It's a king-size bed. You and Max can share it. I'll take the couch." We both know that my couch is one of those uncomfortable-looking modern affairs, and I hope to God she doesn't make me actually sleep on it. Besides, I'm six-foot two, and I'm pretty sure it's only like five-feet long. That would suck. But it would suck worse knowing this angel was in my bed, and I was all alone out in the living room.

"Pace, you can't be serious. I figured your home was like Colton's with fifteen extra bedrooms, and you wouldn't even know we were here, let alone be inconveniencing you like this."

I know she's two seconds away from pulling the plug on this entire thing, and my brain is working overtime to think of something I can say that will get her to stay. I've never wanted a woman to stay over before—usually I have the opposite problem—I'm trying to get someone to leave. Which is the reason I stopped bringing women home altogether. I didn't need a bed for the things I did with them. Sex in a bed would actually be a novelty at this point. But sex in a bed with Kylie ... somewhere we could linger and explore and...

"Max, no!" Kylie shouts, snapping my attention back into the moment.

Oh, Christ. He's found my supply of condoms in one of the bedside drawers. Max is waving the row of packets around in the air like he's discovered his new favorite toy.

Kylie runs after him, but not before her eyes flash on mine. She's noticed the brand name, and the size—extra-large and her mouth has dropped open into an adorable pouty grin.

Yeah, I'm a big boy. But it's okay, angel, I won't just ram him home all at once, I'll make sure you're nice and slippery first.

When she reaches him, he holds the strip up for her to take. "Mumma," he says.

"No, these aren't Mumma's. They are Pace's."

"Pa-pa," he repeats in an attempt to say my name. Kylie's eyes flash to mine, and my chest gets tight.

"I'll teach you about these much later, little dude." I ruffle his hair and accept the condoms from Kylie's outstretched hand. She's holding them like they're diseased. "Sorry about that." I can't tell if she's mad about him finding my stash, or over the sleeping arrangement I've sprung on her. Either way, I'm off to a rocky start.

"It's fine, it's just a good reminder that you can't be serious about giving us your bed."

"Why's that?" I inquire.

"Where will be you bring your ... *dates*? I don't want Max exposed to that type of thing."

"You have nothing to worry about. I don't bring women here."

She watches me curiously, but she doesn't argue.

It's a start. I place their overnight bags on the ottoman at the foot of the bed. "Master bath is through there." I point to the door that opens from the end of my room. "You're welcome to use anything and make yourself comfortable. Towels are in the cabinet under the sink and extra pillows are in the hall closet."

She nods. "Okay, thank you." Her voice is small, and I'm unsure how to read her.

But I don't stand there pondering it for long, because Max has zipped out the door and Kylie gives chase. I follow behind.

After I make sure they're settled, I head into the kitchen with dinner on my mind. "I don't really have any groceries..." I never have groceries. I eat the majority of my meals out, but she doesn't need to know that. Staying in, alone, at my place is something I rarely do, actually. I get too bored. It's too quiet here. I'd rather go over to Colton's or Collins' place, and I do, most nights of the week. "Are you guys okay with takeout?" I ask.

"Sure, takeout's great," Kylie says.

"Pizza or..." I'd been about to suggest sushi, until it occurs to me that infants probably can't eat sushi.

"Pizza is fine with us. Thank you. Let me just grab my wallet, and I can pay for half."

"Your money is no good here, woman." I treat her to a friendly smile, but my tone is firm, so she'll understand I'm serious. I can provide a safe place for her and her son as well as a meal. I don't know why it's so hard for her to just accept a little help. I get the sense she's not used to leaning on people, but it's still frustrating.

Thankfully, for the rest of the evening, Kylie lets me help with all the tasks that require two hands, like cutting up Max's pizza into small bites and screwing the lid on his sippy cup. But she watches me intently the entire time, as if she's trying to figure out my angle. I thought I'd already made that perfectly clear—I told her I liked her. I normally wasn't so forward with my feelings, but she made me act differently. And I was only fully starting to understand that.

KYLIE

I need a moment.

In between Pace suggesting we play house, Max finding his treasure trove of condoms, and discovering what my brain already instinctually knew—that the man was hung like a stallion, and not to mention the bed situation—I am overwhelmed. I'm tired. I'm crabby. And my arm hurts.

I can't believe Pace was really willing to give up his bed for us. When I questioned him about it, he'd shrugged me off like it was no big deal. I don't know what to make of his comment about not bringing women home.

Even as sore as I am, I'm determined to care for Max on my own, if only to prove that I can. If things get awkward here, I need to know I can go home and be fine. Plus it scares me to count on someone. I don't want to need someone who isn't going to stick around. I don't want to have to depend on somebody only to have them leave a hole when they leave.

After changing Max's diaper and wrestling him into pajamas, I laid him down in the center of Pace's big bed and surrounded him by a mountain of pillows. Then I grabbed my cell phone and snuck into the adjoining master bath to call my friend Rachel. I need a moment to myself—to vent or to get advice—I'm not sure.

"Hey Kylie," she answers. "How are you, mama bear?"

"Not great, actually," I admit, sinking to the edge of the large spa tub.

"Talk to me, babe. How's Max? Teething again?"

"No, actually. Max is great. It's me who's a mess." I relay the key points of my current predicament to her.

"Why am I just now hearing about this man?"

"That's your question? I tell you I have a broken arm and that I'm not sure I should be staying here and that's what you want to know about?"

"Of course I want to know about him, because clearly you've been keeping something from me if you're close enough to a man that he's taken you and Max into his home. Who is he? How did you meet him?"

"He's my boss's little brother."

"Little, huh?" she asks. I can hear the smirk in her tone.

"Trust me, there is nothing little about him." I hadn't exactly meant to say that out loud, but Rachel's answering snort tells me that I had.

"He invited you to stay, so what's the problem? Why are you overthinking this?"

"I don't want Max to be confused about who this man is in our lives when I don't even know the answer to that question."

"He's one year old, Kylie. You don't need to have all the answers. Besides, you're allowed to have male friends."

"I suppose so." Logically, her argument makes sense, but it doesn't mean I am comfortable with it.

"You shouldn't worry so much, it causes premature age lines."

I laugh, it's a much needed break in the tension, and feels good. Friends. I could be friends with Pace. Couldn't I? I scrub my hands through my hair. Why does this all feel so overwhelming? "I don't want to give Pace the wrong impression by agreeing to stay here. He's probably going to think this is some kind of casual hook up."

"A man who invites a woman with a child into his home isn't looking for a casual hookup, Kylie," Rachel says.

He's not? But this is Pace.

"Is he hot?" she asks next.

"What? I don't know."

"Of course you do. Use those green eyes of yours. Is he attractive?"

"Y-yes," I stammer. I feel warm and frustrated, and I'm not sure why.

"Then presumably he has no problems getting laid. And a woman with a baby isn't casual hookup material. No offense, honey," she finishes.

"None taken." My days of casual flirting and innocent hookups were over. I have bigger responsibilities now. "So what should I do?"

"Do you feel safe around him?"

"Yes," I answer. "Unequivocally."

"Okay, then. I think you should stay and accept the help. You know I'd invite you over here, but it's a bit of a circus."

"I know. It's fine." Rachel shares an apartment, in typical LA style, with three other girls and one guy. The place isn't overly large to begin with, and it's always a mess. No thank you.

"I wish I could help."

"No worries, we're doing okay. I better get back out there before he realizes I'm hiding in his bathroom."

"You do that. But Kylie, would it really be the worst thing in the world to have some fun with an attractive man?"

Reading between the lines, she's telling me to pull the stick out of my ass and live a little. "I'll consider it," I say.

"And one more thing, you do realize you have the world's cutest baby, right?"

"I do." Max looks just like Elan, who was an attractive man, but Max is a cute as they come. Big, bright blue eyes, but with olive skin and dark hair—nothing like my pale skin and auburn hair. The only downside is that looking at him is a constant reminder of the man who left. As horrible as it sounds, it's also made me wonder if another man could really love my son. He doesn't look like me. If he loves me, but doesn't see Max as a part of me, how does that work? It's a thought that occupies my brain late at night. Pace seems to like Max just fine. I know Rachel would tell me I'm being foolish and to quiet my inner self-doubts. "We'll talk soon," I say, rising to my feet.

When I head back out to the living room, Pace has cleaned up the plates from dinner and is sitting on the sofa with a bottle of beer in one hand and the remote control in the other.

"Is he down?" Pace asks, looking up and locking eyes with me.

"Yes, he's asleep. Are you sure you're okay with us taking your bed?" I ask.

"Of course. I wouldn't have offered if I didn't mean it."

I nod. I'm beginning to understand that about him—he doesn't do or say things just to impress. There is meaning and depth behind everything he does.

"I know you said you don't drink much, but there's more beer, if you want one."

"I'm fine, thanks." I sit down beside him, realizing that the last time we were alone on a couch, I mounted him like a horse and rode him. No, I certainly don't need to add alcohol to the equation. Geez, I'd be bucking against him like a bronco.

"I think I'm going to call it a night," I say, stifling a yawn. It's only eight o'clock, but the meds I took earlier have made me sleepy.

Pace's eyes drift from the television over to me, and he slowly surveys my body. "Are you going to need help getting in and out of that contraption?"

I glance down at myself. I have a cast and a sling over the top of that, holding my right arm still and against my body. Honestly, changing clothes and showering is probably going to be difficult to do one-armed, but I will manage somehow. My cheeks flame bright red just thinking about Pace's big hands moving against my skin to help me disrobe. "I-I'll be okay."

"Suit yourself," he says, his low voice rumbling in the silent room.

"Good night." I want to thank him again for his hospitality, knowing Max is sleeping peacefully in the other room and that we're safe and taken care of for the night makes my chest feel tight. But I tip my head to the floor and scurry off to the bedroom. After checking on Max, I grab a pair of pajamas from my bag and head into the bathroom to change.

I push my arms through the holes of my T-shirt and remove it. My bra comes off next, getting momentarily stuck against my cast, before I free it and toss it aside with my shirt. If I'd known I was going to break my arm today, I wouldn't have worn my skintight skinny jeans. These are hard to remove on a good day. Crap.

I get the jeans halfway down my thighs and begin to shimmy my hips, hoping the move will somehow coax these babies down my legs. No luck. I push and tug and twist, but they are stuck. Placing one foot on the side of the tub, I buck against the fabric.

Shiiiit.

With my legs bound tightly in denim, I tumble to the floor with a shout.

PACE

I sprint down the hall, wondering what the hell could have caused Kylie to scream. My first thought is an intruder. I burst through the door to the bedroom, ready to defend her, but Max is asleep in the bed alone, so then I shove my way into the bathroom.

Kylie is sprawled out on the tile floor, a pair of jeans midway around her thighs, holding her arm to her chest. Her very naked chest. My brain short-circuits temporarily as the abundance of pale, creamy skin hits me.

"Shit, what happened?" I lift her to her feet.

She's breathing and not bleeding anywhere that I can see, but my eyes assess every inch of her, seeking out injury. All I discover is that she has a glorious rack. Full, bouncy C's tipped with tight pink nipples, and my dick springs to life. Her panties are lime green and are the boy shorts kind. They're cute and unexpected.

"A little help here?" she huffs out, flinging her arms across her chest to cover her breasts.

"Sorry. Of course." I sit her down on the edge of the tub and peel the jeans down her legs, freeing her. "There. How's that?"

"Better. Thank you."

She's thanking me for taking her pants off? "Anytime."

We stand there, me with an erect cock, and her dressed in only a pair of panties that show the bottom of her ass cheeks, just watching each other.

"You can go now," she says, her voice small.

There's no way in fuck I'm leaving just when things are getting good. "Come on. Let me help, I won't have you risk further injury." My dimples give away my good mood, but seeing her topless makes me happy.

To my surprise, she doesn't argue. I grab her pajamas from the bathroom counter. I hold the shorts out for her to step into and she places her good hand against my bicep, momentarily uncovering those beauties while she steps one foot and then the other into the shorts. She covers her breasts once again. *No, no, no, that won't do.*

I hold the T-shirt out. "Arms up."

"No way. You'll see my breasts."

"I already saw them, angel and they're perfect, so you have nothing to be self-conscious about." Shit, I'd be tugging on my dick later to the image of them swaying when she moved.

She swallows and slowly lowers her arms.

Hell. Yes.

If she wasn't hurt, I'd want to nuzzle my face right in between them, bath them in kisses, spend hours, no days, getting to know them on a deep, intimate level. I push her arms through the sleeves, and my hands accidentally graze her tits as I lower the shirt.

Kylie sucks in a breath and holds it. "Thank you," she squeaks out a moment later.

"You're welcome," I murmur, my voice thick with desire.

I pray that she'll invite me into the bed with her and Max. I know nothing will happen, I just want to be close to her, but she says goodnight, then closes the bedroom door. My bedroom. That I've willingly given up to her and her child. I don't know who this man is I've become, but I think I like him.

Chapter Seven

KYLIE

In the morning, I wake to the sounds of baby squeals in the distance, and I jump out of bed. Max must have climbed from the bed and is doing God knows what in Pace's condo.

When I reach the living room, the bright sunlight streaming through the huge picture windows tells me it's late morning. Where is Pace? Where is my son?

I head toward the sound of laughter, and I find them in the kitchen. Max is covered in flour and smears of what looks like pancake batter around his mouth.

They are in their own world, laughing, babbling, and cooking together. Pace is heating a skillet on the cooktop and Max is playing with plastic takeout containers and rubber utensils on the floor. They've yet to notice me.

The clock on the microwave tells me it's already 10:30. I haven't slept in this late in over a year. I feel well-rested and calm. Wow. It's crazy what a full night's sleep will do for you. Especially given that my arm is healing.

"Morning," I murmur.

"Hey sleepyhead, " Pace grins up at me with his adorable crooked smile, and my belly does a somersault.

I'd charged out here in a panic, looking for Max—who is totally fine—without giving a thought to my appearance. My curly hair gets crazy while I sleep, and I'm dressed in an old band T-shirt and my short shorts. The pajamas that Pace dressed me in after discovering me naked and sprawled on his bathroom floor. Oh dear God, memories of last night's embarrassment come rushing back to me, along with a healthy dose of shame.

Pace's eyes wander over my body lazily, like he's remembering it in its full sprawled-out glory.

"What are you guys doing?" I ask. It's obvious they're making pancakes, but I just need to get the attention off my bare legs and nipples that are trying to poke through the shirt.

"When I heard him stir this morning, I went in and got him, hoping we could let you sleep in a little. I figured that wasn't something you got to do very often."

He's right, of course. "How long have you guys been up?"

His lips pout in a thoughtful expression while he considers it. "Since 7:30, I think?"

"Oh, he needs a diaper change." I start toward Max.

"Already taken care of," Pace says pouring batter into the sizzling skillet. "I gave him some dry cereal too when he woke up. Wasn't sure how hungry he'd be."

I've never been rendered quite so useless… I don't know what to do with myself, standing in his kitchen in my pajamas. It's disorienting.

"How does your arm feel?" Pace asks.

I hold it out and rotate it around. Other than the cast being annoying and itchy, it's fine. "It feels alright."

"Good," Pace says.

Max has only glanced up at me, hardly acknowledging my presence, and is content to play independently on the floor with the kitchen implements Pace has given him.

"Morning, bubs." I lean down and kiss his head.

He looks up and gives me a gummy grin. "Mumma…"

"I hope he hasn't been too much trouble." My eyes cut to Pace's again.

He looks absolutely delectable in the morning, I decide. His short hair is messy and he's wearing gray athletic shorts and a white-tee. His long feet are bare and every part of him is casual and sexy.

"This little guy? He's a piece of cake," Pace says, pulling me from the visual inspection of his body I'd been indulging in.

My skin warms. "He's not always so easy." I have no idea why I'm trying to warn him away. But he needs to understand what he's stepping into.

"I don't mind, Kylie. I will take care of both of you." His tone is firm, and the expression in his eyes is so sincere, so intense that I know we're no longer just talking about sleepovers, complete with breakfast. His deeper meaning about wanting to take care of us both slams into me and makes my stomach tighten. "Pancakes will be ready in a few minutes," he adds.

"Anything I can do to help?"

"Nope. We got this."

"Okay, I think I'll just go change."

After breakfast, the day went on much the same. Pace was attentive and sweet, and Max seemed content—happy with the extra attention he was receiving from not one, but two caregivers.

I knew Pace would be going back to work tomorrow, but so far, neither of us had mentioned me leaving. He even went to the grocery store and stocked up, saying he wanted to make sure we had enough food for breakfasts and lunches. I could only assume he meant during the workweek when he was gone.

Being here alone during the day would be no different than being alone at my own house, but if I stayed here, at least I'd have help in the evenings, and that was when Max was at his most difficult.

I could still work via my laptop when Max was napping—whether I was here or at home. And there was something comforting about knowing I wouldn't be alone at night.

As a single mother, living alone, I sometimes felt vulnerable, and I knew I would even more so with my right arm in a cast.

***

By dinnertime, I'm feeling eager to earn my keep and decide to treat Pace to my homemade marinara sauce. I make awesome pasta sauce. It's my super power. I tell myself it has nothing to do with impressing this man. It's just a luxury to have the time to actually prepare a nice meal, something more elegant than sandwiches, so I take full advantage. And with Max playing quietly in the living room while Pace watches him, I'm able to devote the time to chopping garlic and onions and simmering tomato sauce.

I hum quietly while I work, enjoying the moment of solitude and the occasional sounds of baby giggles and masculine laughter that drift in from the living room. Doing everything one-handed takes extra time, but that's fine with me.

When everything's finished, I peek my head into the living room. "Pasta's ready," I call out to the guys.

Pace is lying on the living room floor, and Max is climbing his body like it's his personal jungle gym. A brief flash of jealousy flares inside me. I am usually the one to fill this role. But moments later, Pace enters the kitchen with Max on his hip, my heart warms at the sight of them.

"It smells great in here."

I get the sense his kitchen hasn't seen this much action in a while. The only thing in his fridge when we'd arrived were bottles of imported beer and questionable takeout containers, along with a few lingering odors.

I prepare Max's plate first, allowing it to cool while Pace and I fix bowls of pasta for ourselves. I'm pleased to see he takes a large portion.

Once we're all seated at the table, I watch for Pace's reaction as he takes his first bite. "Well?" I ask.

His eyes drift closed, and he groans low in his throat. "Goddamn, woman."

My smile is wide and immediate. "You like it?"

"Very much so," he confirms. "This is incredible."

I try a bite, and I have to agree. Pace stocked his cabinets with authentic olive oil and imported stewed tomatoes from Italy, and you can taste the difference in the quality of the ingredients.

Even Max seems pleased, he shovels big bites of pasta into his mouth, using both fists. Without a highchair, meal times have been interesting. And messy. But Pace doesn't seem to mind, and since it's his home, I let it go too.

"You know that I work for your brother, but you've never told me what it is you do for a living," I say to Pace. Sitting in his beautiful home, watching him enjoy a home-cooked meal, suddenly I'm curious to know more about this man.

"I'm a real estate investor. I find inexpensive or rundown properties and buy them, turning a nice profit after they're fixed up and sold. I have plenty of money to provide for a family, and a flexible enough schedule to actually enjoy one."

"Oh, God, that's embarrassing. That's not at all why I was asking." I want to bury my face in my hands.

"I know that. Don't be embarrassed. I told you that because it's something I want you to know."

"Okay." I don't know how I'm supposed to feel about this information. With every passing glance I can feel deeper meaning and emotion seeping out of him. Everything I know about Pace warns me to stay away. He's a young, wealthy playboy who enjoys sex and likely has several women on the side. But in every interaction with me, and with my son, and especially now being here in his home, where I feel comfortable and at ease, my mind is confused. My physical attraction to him is off the charts, but somehow, with every hour we spend together, it's turning into something more than just physical attraction. I do not know how to handle that information. I'd sealed my heart off a long time ago, afraid I couldn't weather another crushing blow like the one Elan delivered. Yet, there's a tiny voice inside of me whispering that I should go for it. I'm not a big drinker, but suddenly I'm wishing for a glass of wine.

As if reading my mind, Pace rises from the table and retrieves a bottle of red wine from a rack across the kitchen. "I've been saving this for a special occasion, but something tells me it'd pair nicely with the pasta."

He holds up the bottle for my inspection. "What do you think? We still have to get your mini ready for bed..."

"Why do you call him that? No one thinks he looks anything like me."

"Because he is. He's part of you. I can see it in his mannerisms, hear it in his laugh, in his enthusiasm for spaghetti." He smiles at me warmly.

He has no way of knowing it, but everything he's just said cuts to the heart of me. I shrug. "One couldn't hurt."

"Cool." Pace pours us each a glass of red wine and helps himself to a second serving of pasta before rejoining us at the table.

I smile into my napkin. His second serving cements the fact that he really does like my cooking. I think I've had a chip on my shoulder ever since serving him cold grilled cheese. I've redeemed myself in some small way.

By the end of the meal, Max is covered from chin to eyebrows in red pasta sauce.

I try first with paper towels, wiping him down as best I can. "Geez, buddy, how'd you get it in your ears?" I ask Max.

Pace looks on with amusement twinkling in his dark blue eyes. "Shall we just take him out back and hose him off?" he laughs, watching my futile attempts.

"You have a tub, right?" His large jetted tub in the master bath has probably been used for sex, hell, maybe even an orgy, but I'm guessing it's never seen the type of action I have in mind.

"Sure do."

We all three tramp off to the bathroom, the dishes and glasses of wine forgotten on the table.

While Pace adjusts the water and fills the tub, I strip an enthusiastic Max down right there on the bathroom floor. There's just something about a naked baby, with chubby little butt cheeks—complete with dimples— that puts me in a good mood. He's too cute.

We sit together on the bathroom floor while Max splashes and squeals. When I quietly explain to Max that we didn't pack any bath toys, Pace disappears momentarily and returns with an armful of plastic Tupperware containers from the kitchen and dumps then in the tub. Max has a blast filling the cups and bowls with water and dumping them out again. My child is easily entertained.

"So, do you want more kids?" Pace asks.

Whoa. What? "Um, I don't know." One is all I can handle at the moment. Besides, the right man would have to come along first.

"I've always wanted two boys," he continues. "If I have a girl, she'll have me wrapped around her finger so bad." He lifts his pinky into the air and smiles.

I'm unsure how to respond, so I continue watching Max splash. After soaping up all his bits and parts, Pace lifts him, dripping wet from the tub and carries him in a towel to the bed. There I diaper and dress him in the footie-pajamas Pace has gathered. Pace lends a hand as needed, but seems to understand that even though I'm functioning with one arm, I'm not ready to give up complete control.

"Damn, I need a pair of these," Paces says, admiring the footie-pajamas.

My giggle bursts from my mouth uninvited. Just picturing Pace wearing a one-piece pajama outfit has me in stitches. "Sorry." I hold up one hand, trying to regain my composure.

"What? You don't think I could pull off footie-pajamas?" His trademark lopsided grin tugs at something inside me. Oh God, this man is trouble.

Since Max is already yawning and tugging at his ears, I decide to go ahead and tuck him into bed early.

I lay beside him in Pace's big bed and read him the books we've packed. Pace sits at the edge the bed and watches me. Max begins drifting off on my second read through of *Goodnight Moon*. We say goodnight to a bowl full of mush, and a quiet old lady whispering hush, and I repeat again and again, *goodnight moon* until he's sound asleep.

Pace's gaze hasn't strayed from me. I could feel him watching me all through the story, and I'm unsure what it means.

With Max resting quietly between us, Pace and I, as if by silent agreement, each lay down too.

I feel warm and content, laying here with this man and my child. Pace's eyes linger on mine.

We're separated by a sleeping baby, with a good three feet of distance between us, yet somehow I've never felt closer to someone. I decide that tonight I will be bold, and if something happens between us, then I'm ready.

"Goodnight, moon," I whisper to Pace, setting the book down beside us.

"I'm not ready for the night to end yet," he says and the butterflies in my belly take flight.

Chapter Eight

Kylie and I lay there quietly, listening to the soft sucking noises Max makes in his sleep with his pacifier. Lying here with her son between us is much more intimate than any date I've been on. We're growing close. All three of us. I know in this moment that none of the shit I've done—the thrills I've sought, the pleasure I've chased after—has brought me as much joy as being here with her does.

This is true intimacy. I might be one of the more experienced men on the planet, considering I've had more sexual partners than I can count, have tried pretty much everything you could dream up and yet, this is by far, the most sensual moment I've shared with a woman.

She doesn't need me, doesn't need taking care of, and that only makes me want to care for her more. She's the complete opposite of the desperate, clingy women I'm used to.

I watch the pulse thrum in her neck, and I can feel the warmth of not one, but two little bodies next to me, two bodies I want to protect and provide for. I've never felt this way about anyone or anything. I've thought about kids before, but I never imagined it could be like this, that it could stir up so much emotion and longing in me. *She's so capable and self-sufficient, what can I really offer her that she can't provide herself? Pleasure. I can give her pleasure like she's never experienced... I just need for her to give me a shot...*

I remember back to that kiss we shared on her couch. The little sound of pleasure she made when my mouth took hers just about undid me. It was as though she'd been starved for affection. I wanted to give her whatever she wanted. I still do. Sexual tension is thick in the air around us—it has been all day—only neither of us has acknowledged it.

I watch her in the fading light, noticing the way her hair curls softly on my pillow and the way her eyelashes flutter when she blinks. She is mesmerizing.

"You miss it, don't you?" I ask.

"What?" she whispers.

"Sex. Being with a man."

She swallows abruptly, her gaze falling from mine. But she doesn't answer, so I press on.

"Feeling him fill that place deep inside of you. The brush of his lips against yours. That perfect moment when he enters you and steals your breath."

"Pace…"

"You're the one who straddled me like you wanted a good, hard ride. I'm just thinking maybe I could help you out in that area."

"How generous of you." Her tone is sarcastic, but her lips are curved into a grin. "What are you suggesting?" she asks, the pulse in her neck gaining speed.

"You know how I feel, Kylie." My eyes lock on hers and I wait, letting the moment build.

Her breathing grows fast, but she's still and quiet. "What about Max?" We both look down at the little one sleeping soundly between us.

"Come with me." My voice comes out rougher than I intend, and filled with need.

We rise quietly from the bed, and I'm debating where to take her. The living room is out. We need a door—with a lock. I briefly consider the bathroom—or more specifically, the shower, then decide I need more room to maneuver than that.

I lead her into my office and shut and lock the door behind us. When I turn to face Kylie, she's trembling all over. I stalk closer, pushing her back up against the door and lean in to inhale her scent. Warm vanilla, along with traces of baby boy. If I weren't so damn aroused, I'd laugh.

I can feel her heart slamming against her ribcage. She's as tense as a cobra about to strike.

"Breathe for me, angel," I remind her.

She draws a deep breath into her lungs.

I bring my hands to her cheeks and lift her face to make sure she's meeting my eyes. I need to see her eyes to know she understands what's about to happen. My thumbs lightly caress her skin, and I speak in hushed tones, slowly, letting my meaning sink in. "I know you said you're not ready for more, and I know you worry about Max. But clearly you need someone you can count on. If you're sure this can't go further, at least let me be there for you. I can be a friend—a friend who supplies mind blowing orgasms, if you like."

"This sounds like friends with benefits."

"I promise you that I fuck better than any man you've been with. Aren't you curious to see for yourself?"

I know I'm pushing her—but something tells me I have to in order for us both to get what we want. She's so used to being in control all the time, relying only on herself for every decision. Well fuck that, I'm taking this decision out of her all-too-logical head. I'm letting her body decide. And judging by the way her nipples have hardened, and her pulse thrums at the base of her throat—her body wants this. Plus, I truly believe she wants a good, hard fuck every bit as bad as I do. And hell, if that was the thing that got her to see how good we could be together if she just gave me the chance, then I'd gladly sacrifice my body for the greater good.

She draws in a shuddering breath and chews on her lower lip. "You were right about one thing."

"What's that?" I ask, dropping my voice lower as I read the consent in her eyes.

"It has been too long."

"You want to feel my cock inside you, angel?" I press my hips forward, letting her feel that I'm already hard.

She lets out a tiny sound of pleasure from the back of her throat. "Is this all you want? Just sex?" she asks, blinking up at me with solemn green eyes.

"He might have thrown you away, but I'm not going to do that." The truth is I want her. All of her, including her son. And by some small coincidence, the universe had supplied me with the perfect opportunity for me bringing her home. It sucks that she broke her arm, but it gave me the opportunity I needed to bring her home and show that I could and would take care of her.

"Trust me, okay?"

She nods.

It's a start.

I take her mouth, kissing her long and deep, my tongue stroking hers, tasting the wine we shared earlier.

"God, you have no idea how sexy you are." I push my hips into hers again.

"Me? Sexy?" She looks down at herself and almost laughs. "Yes, because a T-shirt and yoga pants are the epitome of sex appeal. Throw in my usual unwashed hair in a messy ponytail, and we have the trifecta."

Watching her round ass move and sway in stretchy yoga pants all day was almost too much. "Your body is beautiful—never doubt that." My stare latches onto hers and after a few moments, she gives a quick nod.

I don't know what she's so afraid of. I am nothing like that asshole ex of hers. I can't ever imagine walking away from her or Max. I don't care that he's not biologically mine. He's part of Kylie, and that's all that matters

A crease lines her forehead, and I know she's lost in her head again, over-analyzing every detail of me and her together. I smooth the line with my thumb. "Stop thinking so much," I whisper.

She nods and brings her mouth to mine. I kiss her deeply, exploring her mouth and sucking on her tongue. Then I kiss all the way down the side of her throat, moving lower. Kylie groans and pushes her free hand into my hair, encouraging the contact.

"That's it, angel. Let it go." I can feel her relaxing, relinquishing the control I desire over her body, her head, her heart.

After spending the day watching her cook in my kitchen, and listening to her sweet voice as she sang familiar, yet long-forgotten songs to Max? There is something I like about it. Something *real*. I have no desire to hit the bar scene and seduce a girl with the same words I've used a thousand times. Uttering the phrases I know will make her lick her lips and follow me wherever I want to go, which was most likely to a bathroom or my car, since I had no desire to bring a random hookup into my home. Entering her pussy rhythmically until I came, without any care or concern for her orgasm.

Kylie is so different. None of my standard operating procedures apply, and the chase is new and thrilling.

"Pace, I don't know what I'm doing… This isn't me," she says, pulling my thoughts back into the moment.

"Trust me, I love that," I admit. Her eyes find mine and she releases a little sigh. "Can you do one thing for me?" I ask, sensing she's right on the edge. She's on the verge of pulling away from me. And I don't want that.

"Yes," she murmurs.

"Let me make you come. I need my mouth on you. And then you can decide if you want anything else to happen."

She considers it, only for a brief moment, her eyes dropping to the floor between us and then rising to land on mine again. "Yes, okay," she says.

That's my girl. Pride bursts through me. I know this is big for her—she's taking a chance not just with her body, but with her heart.

"What about you?" she asks, as I slip my hand into the front of her yoga pants and lightly touch her over her panties.

My needs in this equation? "Not important," I say, kissing the side of her neck while my hand slides lower. Of course my hope is that she'll see how good we could be if she'd just let herself lose some of that tight control. This is my way of showing her that I'm not just some selfish prick, in or out of the bedroom. Her needs will come first. And I will be here for her.

Still kissing and gently biting the side of her neck, I push my fingers into the side of her panties and find them damp. My dick pulses in my jeans. He likes this information. I stroke her lightly and feel her breath shudder. Her tissues are swollen and wet. *Fuck, yes.* I love that I get her wet and wanting, even though her head isn't so sure about this.

Unlike the last time, I don't want us to feel rushed. I'm desperate to see her creamy, pale skin and full breasts that I got a glimpse of last night. Reluctantly pulling my fingers from her panties, I feel a frustrated groan rise from her chest.

I systematically strip her naked— kissing each bit of skin I expose. Her breasts, her stomach, the tops of her thighs, and finally when her panties join the rest of her clothes on the floor, I take a second just to appreciate how fucking fine she is.

She fidgets, pressing her thighs together and lifting her arms like she wants to cover herself. I grip her wrist and shake my head. No fucking way. Kylie chews on her lower lip, but doesn't say anything.

I walk her backwards to the desk and lift her so she's sitting right on the edge. I drop one more kiss on her lips, and then sink to my knees. Parting her thighs wide, I press closer and kiss her lower stomach, right above her mound. When I glance up, I notice she's closed her eyes. Hell no. I want her to know

I'm the one giving her this pleasure. "Open them," I command.

Her eyes flash on mine.

"I want you to watch," I say, my tongue licking lazily up her silken folds while my eyes stay glued to hers.

Her eyelids flutter, but they remain open as she tracks the movements of my tongue. Up and down, I tease her, slowly at first, letting her get warmed up. Her pussy is every bit as beautiful as the rest of her. Neatly trimmed, nice and pink. If she thought she was undesirable, then she was insane. Every inch of her is perfection as far as I can tell. And the crazy thing is, as gorgeous as she is, it's really her heart—the soft, nurturing side she's given me a glimpse of—that really steals my breath.

Tiny whimpers escape her lips, and her breathing grows fast.

"Don't take your eyes off of me," I growl.

Kylie refocuses her attention at the spot between her thighs that I'm intent on worshipping. I lick against her clit in a brutal rhythm. I have to physically restrain her, holding her hips in place, so she can't squirm away. She's close, I can tell, and when I plunge two fingers deep into her heat and curl them up to meet her special spot, she comes on command, bucking against me and clawing her fingers through my hair. My dick salutes her show. It seems impossible, but she is even hotter when she comes, and the urge to do this with her every day spikes within me.

When I rise to my feet, she's looking at me with lust-filled eyes. Wordlessly, she attempts to unbuckle my belt, but fumbles with it one-handed, I reach down to help her and once my jeans are open, she reaches into my jeans.

Shit.

Her hand is soft and delicate compared to mine and my cock immediately takes notice, hardening to steel and weeping for her.

She jacks me up and down while I take her mouth, kissing her deeply so she can taste how sweet she was on my tongue.

"Kylie, you don't have to," I choke out, even though I don't want her to stop.

"I want to," she breathes against my lips.

Fuck yeah.

I help her, shoving my jeans down my hips until my cock is free.

"Do you wear boxers?" she asks.

"Not usually," I admit.

"God, Pace."

I look down, trying to understand the panic in her voice.

She's holding my cock away from my body like she's inspecting it.

What in the hell?

"Are you serious?" she asks, her mouth curling up in a devilish grin.

"About?"

"This thing is massive."

I notice her fingers don't close around me, and I chuckle darkly, pride tearing through me.

"I mean, I know I've had a baby, but I'm actually scared right now."

I take her face in my hands again. "I told you we won't do anything you don't want to. But I promise you, it will fit if you want to do that."

She swallows down her fears and nods up at me. Then she takes me by complete surprise, dropping down from the desk, and lowering herself to her knees before taking me in her mouth.

I reach out blindly, gripping the edge of the desk. Christ, her mouth is like a vacuum. She sucks me in deeply, creating a warm suction all around me. She strokes my base with one hand while her mouth goes to work. Even one-handed, her touches feel incredible. She reaches down to lightly grip my nuts. *Goddamn.* I shudder. Most women don't know how to handle the sensitive areas of a man's body, but Kylie does. She gently tugs on the hyper-sensitive globes before releasing her suction on my cockhead to lick them. I cannot control the groan that tears from deep within my throat. One thing is certain, Kylie gives one hell of a blow job.

"Fuck, angel." I reach down and smooth her hair back from her face while she eagerly grins up at me with a mouthful. "That feels amazing."

After a few more wet kisses strategically placed in spots that make me groan, I help her rise to her feet. She glances down at my cock and then back up at me in a way that says, *It's time to put that big thing to use.* Yes, ma'am.

I consider bending her over my desk, since I've been tortured by her beautiful round ass all day, but I know that the first time I have her, I need to see her eyes. It's never been something important to me until right this moment. It should scare me, but I feel calm and in control.

Taking her in my arms, I lift her to the edge of the desk again and spread her thighs so I can step in between them. Yanking my shirt off over my head, I also let my jeans drop to the floor and step out of them. I want to feel her skin against mine.

Her eyes lower, travelling down my chest and abs before rising again. I like the small smile I see playing on her lips. She reaches out and circles her hand around my cock, looking up at me in wonder, like she can't believe this is really about to happen.

I lift her chin and kiss her again, then pull back to meet her eyes. "I'll be careful with you, always. I promise." We both know I'm not just talking about sex—I'm referring to her emotions.

She nods.

I line myself up against her heat and gently rub back and forth. Kylie shudders and arches her back, ready to take me.

"Fuck, a condom," I groan. I'd almost forgotten. That's never happened before.

"Are you clean?" she asks.

"Of course. I never fuck without a condom."

She hesitates just a moment as though reading me. I've told her before that I'd never lie to her, and I can tell she's recalling that. "I'm on birth control," she says.

Bareback? With this beautiful woman? I'm certain I'll come too fast and embarrass myself without the layer of latex between us, but I don't care. I want to feel her. Just her.

Without a piece of rubber between us. "Are you sure?"

She quickly nods and reaches for me again. "Yes, I'm sure."

I position her so that her casted arm rests comfortably between us, being careful not to jostle it too much. "I don't want to hurt you," I say.

"I'm fine, Pace. I promise."

I ease forward, keeping one hand on the base of my shaft and one hand on her hip as our bodies join. The wet heat that envelopes me is indescribable. Inch by inch, I bury myself inside her. Fuck.

Kylie's whimper once I'm fully seated makes my balls tighten.

"How does that feel?" I choke out.

Her eyes lift to mine. "My vagina isn't stretched out."

"What?"

"My ex ... he said he didn't want to be with a woman who was fat and had a stretched out vagina after having a baby."

"As much as I love discussing your ex while I'm inside you, what are you talking about, angel?"

"My vagina—it feels normal. It doesn't feel stretched out."

"It feels fucking awesome." I still my movements and look deep into her eyes. "And you're nowhere near close to fat. Your body did something fucking amazing. You grew a little person in there. With all due respect to Max's father, he sounds like a fucking moron."

Kylie smiles up at me, placing her palm against my cheek.

I take that as a signal that sharing time is over, and it's time to get down to business. Which is excellent news, because if I don't move soon I'm going die.

I lift her calves, securing both of her ankles around my back. "Hang on, baby."

Kylie grips my shoulder with her good hand, and with my hands still holding her legs, I begin sliding in and out once again. She moans softly and digs her fingernails into my back. It feels incredible. I love watching her take her pleasure while I fuck her. She tightens her legs around my waist, arching into my thrusts to take me deeper and her cheeks flush with heat. She is alive and confident. It's incredibly sexy.

I move slowly, pressing deep and then retreating. I want this moment to last.

"Tell me how to make you come. Tell me what you need," I whisper, pressing light kisses to her mouth.

"Harder. I need it harder," she says.

Oh fuck, yeah. Done with holding back, I rock into her, giving her my full length, gaining speed with each thrust until I'm fucking her hard and fast.

Kylie moans softly and her normally bright green eyes glaze over with lust.

I slam into her again and again, barely holding off my own impending orgasm in pursuit of hers.

"Let it go," I remind her again and she does. Her muscles squeeze around me, and she lets out a low whimper, clutching my shoulder and crying out my name.

Pace.

The sound of my name shuddering on her lips undoes me.

I come with a small shout, burying my face into her neck as I spill inside of her.

Chapter Nine

KYLIE

I'm still trembling as I crawl back into bed with Max. I cannot believe what I've done. I not only let Pace fuck me on his office desk, I begged him to do it harder. *Oh dear, God.*

I bury my face in my shaky hands. And worst of all is that I'm still smiling, and I want to do that again and again. I know I've fought it hard and tried to convince myself that this man doesn't fit into our lives, but at every turn, he proves me wrong.

After our intimate encounter in his office, he grabbed a handful of tissues to clean up his essence that was running down my thighs. Then we'd redressed in silence, the weight of what we'd just done sinking in. He kissed me goodnight in the hallway and then headed to the couch while I retreated to the safety and comfort of his bedroom. Which is where I am now.

Max is still sound asleep, thank goodness, oblivious to what just took place.

My cell phone chimes signaling a new text, and even though my limbs are heavy with sleep, and I'm sure it's no one important, I reach blindly toward the bed side table until my fingers close around it.

It's Pace.

Goodnight, Moon.

How two simple words placed together on the screen can make me feel so much, I have no idea. The way his eyes stayed on me while I read the story to Max is a feeling I will never forget. It makes me feel like I'm beautiful, not just as a mother, but as a woman.

I tuck the phone under the pillow and drift off into a peaceful sleep, thankful for Pace's presence in our lives.

Little did I know that everything would change the following day.

***

The morning starts with Pace getting ready for work quietly while Max and I sleep in his bed. Well, Max sleeps and I drift in and out to the sounds of the shower running, to the scent of aftershave wafting from the steam-filled bathroom. I rest quietly with a smile on my mouth remembering last night.

When Pace steps out of the walk-in closet, he's dressed in navy suit pants, and a crisp white shirt with a gray tie. He looks smart, and put together and ready to take on the world. I'm reminded of his proclamation that he could take care of us both—me and Max. I imagine what it would be like to welcome a man like him home every evening. Someone to eat with, play with, and daydream about the future with.

I swallow a lump in my throat at the sudden rush of emotion threatening to overwhelm me.

"You're staying right?" Pace whispers.

I nod. "Yes. What time will you be home?"

"Mondays after work I normally meet my brothers for a drink. It'll just be me and Collins. I can cancel," he says.

"No, go. It's fine. I'm used to this, remember?"

"Yes, but not one-handed, you're not. I'll be home by eight."

We keep our voices low in an attempt not to wake a sleeping Max.

"Okay," I say. "Have a good day."

"You too." He leans down and kisses my forehead, then looks thoughtfully at Max and does the same to him.

He doesn't mention last night, and I don't know what I expected him to say, but the fact that he doesn't acknowledge it at all makes me feel uneasy. Did last night mean as much to him as it did to me?

I want to pull him down onto the bed with me and tell him that last night was amazing, but I don't. Instead, I watch him leave from my warm spot in the bed and wonder what he's thinking.

Later, I shower, careful to keep my cast dry, catch up on some work, and play with Max. But then something strange happens around lunchtime.

Elan calls.

Utterly shocked, I ignore it, but he proceeds to call seven more times.

On the eighth phone call, I pick up, thinking something terrible must have happened. I have no idea why he'd be trying to get ahold of me.

"Hello?"

"Kylie..." His voice is immediately familiar and comforting.

I hate it.

"Elan? What's going on? Has something happened?" I ask, ignoring the feelings that flood my system when he speaks my name.

"Yes." He releases a heavy sigh and pauses. "I've made a terrible mistake."

I listen, waiting for him to continue, my eyes on Max where he plays on the carpet at my feet.

"You, and my ... my son... I..." his voice cracks.

"How did you know it was a boy?" I ask.

"I had a dream. A beautiful dream about you both. I pushed you away because I was afraid, and now I fear it's too late."

I sink down onto the couch. Of course it's too late.

Isn't it?

I want to scream at him, I want to hang up the phone and not give it a second thought, but I'm unable to. For months and months I wanted nothing more than for Elan to come around, to know that someday Max could have a relationship with this man. I've accepted that Elan and I are through, but I never wanted my son to suffer this loss.

I listen, numb, while Elan relays a story to me about his parents and how they lost a baby—a baby meant to be his younger sister—when she was just a newborn, and how the loss was so devastating, so tragic that they never recovered. Not only did their marriage fall apart, but his mother was committed to an institution when he was six years old and remained there for three years.

He tells me all of this and explains that is why he had been terrified of bringing a new baby into this world with me. My brain spins and spins. I hand Max a stuffed animal and make it dance around, but the phone stays glued to my ear, and my brain is elsewhere.

"I want to see you, to meet my son. I want a chance to build back what we had."

"What are you saying? You left us. You sent someone by with a check! You weren't even man enough to come by yourself. To look me in the eye..." I lower my tone, realizing I'm on the verge of screaming and take a deep, calming breath. I stand and pace the room, heading into the kitchen to get some distance from Max's little ears.

"What did you name him?" he asks, his voice whisper-soft unlike I've ever heard it before.

"Maxwell," I say. "But I call him Max." I don't explain that I'd chosen the name as a constant reminder to myself to maximize every moment and to never feel sorry for myself over the situation.

"It's perfect," he says. "Kylie? What do you say? I'd like to meet my son."

I open my mouth to refuse his request, but my eyes wander over to my son—my son who looks exactly like his father and a sense of stillness washes over me. I know that for Max's sake, I need to hear him out. I have no legal right to refuse Elan. It occurs to me that if I try to deny him access to Max, he could get lawyers involved and try to get joint custody. I don't want that.

"I… I don't know, Elan. I've met someone," I say. "I'm happy." The image of Pace's intense gaze as he sunk into me last night, so concerned with my arm, and my pleasure, rips through me making me shiver.

"Please," he begs. "Wouldn't it be best for our son if we were together?"

I tell him that I need time to think, and we end the call.

My mind is playing through various scenarios all day long, but I'm unable to escape that realization that Elan is right about one thing. I owe it to Max to at least talk to Elan. It is best for Max if I give him a fair, fighting chance at a relationship. It will not be easy for him to win my trust back, and I don't even know if he deserves a shot after the way he walked out on me, but it's in Max's best interest. And there is nothing I would not do for my son.

I call him back several hours later.

"Okay," I say. No hello, no formal pleasantries, because I am not in the mood for all the fanfare. I feel like I'm conceding—like I'm giving up a piece of myself. I've had Max all to myself this entire time, so maybe I am. Even if it is the right thing to do for all involved.

"Okay?" he asks.

"You can meet him," I say.

"Today. Are you free?"

Knowing that Pace won't be home until late, I agree. "Okay. The park by my house. I'll text you when Max wakes up from his nap, and we'll head over there."

"I will be there," Elan says, excitement heavy in his voice.

I pull in a deep breath, trying to quiet all of the warring emotions inside of me. "See you then."

***

Elan arrives right on time, hitting the button on his key fob to lock his Mercedes before starting across the park toward us. His eyes immediately stray from mine over to Max. He swallows, nervously and licks his lips. "Wow." He's looking Max over from top to bottom, no doubt amazed at the uncanny resemblance.

Elan looks different. Older somehow. There are little lines around his eyes and more weight around his middle than I remember. He sits quietly on the bench beside me and watches Max plays with a set of trucks I've brought. Max seems pretty oblivious to his presence. Elan seems completely humbled.

He'd arrived empty handed, and I'm not sure what I expected, but I guess it was something more than nothing. Not that gifts would make up for his year-long absence, but maybe it'd be a small token in the right direction—and provide something so that

Max could immediately relate to this new, strange man. Even Pace, bachelor extraordinaire, thought to bring a gift the first time he spent time with Max.

Elan sits with his hands folded in his lap watching Max play and babble. "He's beautiful. Does he say any words?"

"Yes, Mumma and ball are all he says right now, but he knows the signs for lots of things. Eat, milk, more, and all done." I could babble on and on. I want him to understand how amazing Max is and that it's entirely his fault that he chose not to be part of it. I'm still angry, and rightly so, but I'm trying to be open for what is best for my son.

It's a strange sensation knowing I share a child with this man. We made the little being playing between us. I feel uneasy, yet part of me knows that being here today, introducing Elan to his son is the right thing.

It makes me sad realizing how many things Elan has missed. Max's birth, his baptism, his first birthday, his first steps. I blink back tears. At least he's here now. It's going to take a while for him to build a relationship with Max. But then I realize how that's not entirely true. Max and Pace bonded almost instantly. But then again, Pace got right down on the ground and interacted with him. Spoke to him and showed him things. Elan is sitting quietly beside me like he's confused. Maybe he's still in shock.

I don't know why I keep thinking about Pace. As amazing as last night was, I've known from the start his world and mine don't mix. And now that Elan seems like he wants to be back in the picture, I'm more confused than ever.

Chapter Ten

"What's new with you, man?" I ask Collins, tipping the bottle of beer to my lips. We've already covered the topics of work and recent stock market trends. Some emerging fund in Brazil has him all excited, and I'm only too happy to listen while he prattles on. I'm still trying to figure out a way to tell him about Kylie, because of course she's the only thing on my mind. Last night was off the fucking charts. I could barely look at her this morning without getting hard. I'd left pretty quickly to avoid embarrassing myself.

"How's Tatianna?" I ask. I haven't seen her around in a while, though I know as a top model, she travels often for work.

He's gazing over at the musician's warming up at the jazz club he wanted to meet at. It's soon going to be a little too loud for conversation, but maybe that's what he intended. "Everything's good," he says, taking a drink from his glass.

I get the sense there's more he wants to say, so I wait.

He shrugs. "Sometimes, I don't know. I get the sense that all I am to her is a padded bank account, and all she is to me is a warm pussy to sink into."

"I didn't know you were looking for anything serious," I say.

"Yeah, I guess I'm not."

He's not very convincing. He turned thirty this year, and I wonder if that has anything to do with his melancholy mood and rhetorical questions about the nature of his relationship.

When I glance over at Collins, he looks a bit lost. Fuck. I suddenly find myself wishing Colton were here. He would know the right thing to say at a time like this.

"Listen, if you're not happy, you can always break up with her, right?"

"It's not that I'm unhappy. I just wonder if there's something more out there."

"There is," I say with conviction.

"You?" He turns to me suddenly, his mouth curling into a grin. "I didn't ever think I'd see the day, little brother. Who is she?"

"Kylie." Her name alone gives me a warm feeling. Christ, I'm in deep already.

"The girl with the baby who works for Colton?"

She is so much more than just a girl with a baby. Collins doesn't understand, but I know he will once he gets to know her. "Yes. She's the one."

"The one? Wow." His eyes widen.

I hadn't meant it in those terms, but now that the thought is out there, I don't hate it. Shit, I could see it now all laid out before me. Holding her warm body in my arms every night, watching Max grow... I know I'm moving quickly, but this woman is not a flavor of the week. I'm usually a hit it once kind of guy, but with her, that never even crossed my mind. I want more. I want to stick around to see where this can go. It's entirely new and thrilling knowing there is more to discover.

"Do you want to stay and order dinner?" Collins asks, signaling the waitress for another round of drinks.

"Sure, just let me check on Kylie real quick. She broke her arm and is staying at my place."

He raises his brow, but doesn't say anything. I'm sure I'm shocking the hell out of him. I don't even bring hookups over to my place for an hour. Kylie could move in permanently, and I wouldn't bat an eyelash.

How are you holding up?

I wait for her reply with my phone in my hand.

Five minutes pass and nothing. Collins is reading the dinner menu, but my stomach is churning with unease. I dial her number, and it rings repeatedly until her voicemail picks up. I call twice more and still no answer. Something feels off.

"Sorry about dinner, I think I'm going to have to split, man. Kylie's not picking up her phone, and I'm getting worried. I need to make sure something didn't happen to them."

He nods. "Of course. Go. It's fine. We'll do dinner next week when Colton gets back."

"Sure." Distracted, I rise to my feet, throw a couple of bills down onto the table and leave in a panic.

The entire drive home, I curse at myself.

She's got a broken arm for fuck's sake, and I left her alone with a one-year-old. What the fuck was I thinking?

***

I want to fucking punch something. Not only are her and Max gone, but all their bags are too. I have no idea what could have happened in the span of eight hours that caused her to pack up and leave. When I left her this morning, she was curled up in my bed, looking content and happy. I figured she'd be staying put. She told me she would. What changed?

There's still no answer on her cell, and when I drive by her house, her car isn't there. I don't like the thought of her and Max out there alone somewhere. There's a hard knot in my chest and I grip the steering wheel too tight. The only thing to do is go home and wait. But as I'm driving past the park near her house – I spot them.

I park at the curb and climb out of my car.

Kylie is sitting on a bench next to a man and Max is playing in the grass at their feet. Her posture is tense and guarded, and the man at her side is looking at Max with full interest. A million scenarios flash through my head, but the only one that makes sense is that this man is her ex, Max's father. When I get closer, I see he's got the same dark hair and olive skin tone as Max. My stomach cramps up and I stop briefly where I can study them from a distance. Watching her with another man makes me feel more possessive than I have in my entire life. I want to drag her back to my home like some goddamn caveman. But I realize that's not all I want. Standing here, in the presence of this man, I want her to choose *me*. I stop beside them, my eyes burning on Kylie.

"Pace, what are you doing here?" her tone is abrupt, like I've caught her in the middle of something.

I guess I have.

"You weren't answering your phone. I was worried." I don't mention that I also discovered her bags were gone from my place. We will discuss that later, in private.

"I'm fine. We're okay. This is Max's father, Elan." She looks over at the man beside her and my fists curl into tight balls.

"Kylie?"

"It's okay, Pace," she encourages.

I do not know what the fuck is happening, or what alternate universe I've entered into, but this is not okay. This man left her – humiliated her. Sent money, but never gave his time, his love. What in the fuck is she doing here, casually sitting, and talking to him like everything is okay? I make a protective move toward Kylie and Max, the muscles in my jaw twitching.

"Who's this?" Elan asks. "I didn't know you were seeing anyone."

"I'm not," Kylie says, looking straight at me.

Her words cut into the heart of me and my stomach tightens. I feel like fighting someone. Kylie asked before if I often went out and got rowdy, well she was about to find out. But then I realize Max is sitting in the grass, looking up at me adoringly. I head over to him and pet his hair. "Hey little man."

"Pa-pa," he says, moving toward me, his eyes lighting up.

"He's calling this man Papa?" Elan says, the annoyance clear in his voice.

I turn to suddenly, a flash of anger rising up inside me. "You left them," I enunciate each word clearly and slowly. "I've been taking care of them both. You cast them aside like a fool, not seeing their value, and believe me, I'm more than happy to step in and take your son in as my own." Kylie's eyes widen, and she lets out a surprised exhale. But

I'm on a roll now. "*I* will be the one who teaches him how to play catch, and I will be the one who teaches him to surf, how to treat a woman."

"Pace," Kylie interrupts my speech, looking upset. "You should go."

I release a huge exhale, and watch her eyes. She looks scared and hurt and confused, but she stands her ground, her posture straight and sure. Taking a glance down at Max, his little face is a mask of concentration and he looks worried. I see now that I'm not welcome here. I'm interrupting a family reunion and fuck, I've lost my cool in front of Max. That pisses me off more than anything.

I clench my fists and nod once to Kylie. "Will you at least call me later so I know you're safe?"

"Yes," she says.

Defeated, I turn and head for my car.

Chapter Eleven

PACE

Once at home, my condo is empty and lifeless. I throw my keys and phone down on the counter feeling angry and out of control.

That fucker looked so smug, so cool and aloof. He has no idea what he willingly gave up. And now I'm completely fucking confused about what Kylie wants. After last night, I thought that was it. Our relationship was a done deal in my mind. I wanted to move her in permanently. Make her mine. Give Max my last name if that was what she wanted. I'm not a relationship guy, yet I was willing to change my entire world for this woman and another man's child. But now? Now, I have no fucking clue what's going on.

I consider alcohol, but I know I want to be clear headed when Kylie calls later. I need my wits about me. I need to talk some sense into her. She might think Elan is the better choice just because he fathered Max, but I know for certain he's not. Any man who takes off on his pregnant girlfriend isn't worthy of this woman.

I pace my condo as the light fades in the sky and wonder why she hasn't called yet. Finally my cell phone chimes from the counter, and I race to the kitchen.

There's a text from Kylie.

We're home, and I just got Max tucked into bed. Sorry if I caused you any worry today.

If she thinks a single text message is going to be enough after all the heart ache and tension I've felt since discovering she was gone, she's insane.

I press the call button and wait while it rings.

"Hi," she answers, her voice sleepy.

There are so many questions spinning in my head, I don't even know where to start. "Why did you leave?" I ask.

"I'm sorry about that. I didn't mean to just take off without explanation. I want to thank you for your hospitality, but I figured you could use your space back."

The air feels like it's been knocked from my lungs. *My hospitality?* "We fucked bareback last night. Whether or not you believe it, that meant something to me. *You* mean something to me. What the hell is going on, Kylie?"

She sighs softly. "Elan called today. He said that he knew he made a mistake walking out on us, and he wanted a chance to meet Max."

"And you gave in, just like that?"

"He could have taken me to court, Pace. Served me with papers for a custody arrangement. I couldn't have that. So, yes, I was doing what I thought was best. For me and for my son."

Realizing I've wandered into my bedroom, I sink down onto the bed, the phone pressed against my ear, and my heart heavy. "I see." I know I should apologize for my outburst at the park today. I got a little territorial seeing Kylie and Max with another man in the picture. Although, I suppose I don't know if he's truly back, or if it was a one-time thing, him wanting to meet Max. "So, is Elan back?" I ask, even though her answer has the potential to destroy me.

"I don't know for sure. He says he wants a chance with me. A chance to be a real family, but I told him he's a long ways off from me trusting him again."

I swallow a lump in my throat. "And what about you? What do you want?"

She hesitates for a moment and a wave of panic rises inside of me. "I'm trying to put my son first, and I guess deep down, I believe it would be best for Max if Elan and I could work things out."

She's told me all I need to know. Despite her insistence the past several weeks that I'd only end up hurting her, the opposite has happened. She has just gutted me, and I don't think she even knows it.

"You didn't have to leave," I say, trying to regain my composure. "Unless your arm magically healed in the last few hours, I'm guessing you still need the help."

"With me trying to be open to exploring things with Elan, I didn't feel right staying with you. Plus, if I'm honest, I don't think I could trust myself alone with you after what happened last night."

"And what happened last night?" I want to hear it in her own words, I want to know if she feels as strongly about what happened as I do.

"As I told you last night, it had been too long. And the sex was great, if that's what you're wondering."

Of course it felt great, but it was so much more than the physical act. It was her giving herself to me fully, me claiming her as my own. But apparently we are not on the same page. She's not mine. And Max isn't either.

"It was good, wasn't it?" I say, trying to regain some of the cocky bad boy who never lets his heart get engaged.

Kylie's quiet, and I wonder what she's thinking. I want to ask how Max is, how it went when he met Elan for the first time, but I stay quiet too.

Finally, after several seconds of silence, I realize there is nothing more to say. "Goodnight, Moon," I whisper.

"Goodnight," she whispers back.

I lay back against the pillows. The smell of warm vanilla and little boy greets me. My chest tightens and I squeeze my eyes closed, wondering what I'm supposed to do now.

***

Despite the darkness that's settled all around me, despite the quiet, stillness of my home, I am unable to sleep. I lay unmoving for several hours, my head still spinning with everything that's happened in the past twenty-four hours. I can't believe that just last night, I was inside Kylie, watching her come apart, and today she's trying to let me down easy and telling me she's going to make a go at things with her baby's father.

My stomach growls, reminding me that I never had dinner. I head to the kitchen, remembering there are leftovers of the pasta Kylie made last night.

While I wait for the microwave to heat my food, I pick up my phone and call Collins.

I don't bother with pleasantries. I don't bother asking about Tatianna – he seemed so reluctant to discuss their relationship at happy hour, I just launch straight into the hell my last few hours have been.

"Calm down, get yourself under control, man," Collins interrupts my rant.

I take a deep breath.

"What should I do?"

"Don't be a dumbfuck."

"That's your advice, asshole?" I'm about to hang up on him when the sound of his laughter fills the space between us.

"You're a Drake. Figure it out. Go get your girl back."

He's right. Colton didn't let the distance Sophie put between them keep them apart. She flew to Italy to escape him, and shit, he was married at the time. They had more of an uphill battle to wage than Kylie and I do, right? I won't just sit back and let this asshole squeeze his way back into the picture.

I shovel several forkfuls of pasta into my mouth, knowing I'm going to need the fuel, and grab my keys and wallet, then take off out the door.

KYLIE

As I hang up the phone, a wave of nausea hits me, and I'm terrified I'm doing the wrong thing. There is no guidebook on how to be a single mother, or what to do when your baby-daddy calls you unexpectedly. I believed the right thing to do was probably to give him a chance. A chance for Max to have a real family – instead of just me, trying to do it all and barely keeping my head above water. And speaking of doing it all, I've done too much today. My house is clean, and my laundry is caught up, but my arm is sore and achy.

I curl up in bed, laying on my side as visions of last night with Pace flood my brain. He'd been so strong, so commanding with his filthy words and massively large cock, yet tender and sweet at the same time with his concern over my casted arm. Just thinking of him produces a rush of conflicting emotions. I guess it's true what they say about wanting what you can't have. Even though he'd proven himself reliable, part of me still believes that he's too young and too immature to really settle down into the stable type of relationship I need right now.

Tears leak from the corners of my eyes and I hug my pillow to my chest. My heart is heavy and I'm so confused about my path, but I have to believe that if I put Max first, I will make the right decision.

Chapter Twelve

The florescent lights of the twenty-four-hour superstore shine brightly overhead, momentarily disorienting me from my task. I'm staring at a wall display of six different types of outlet covers. Given that it's nearly two in the morning, my eyes are glazed over as I try to read the packages to decipher the differences. Finally settling on one called *Universal Baby Saver*, I toss it in my cart.

My cart is already overflowing. I've gathered soft fleece blankets, teddy bears, balls, trucks, trains that make sounds, an inflatable dragon, because who doesn't need an inflatable dragon? A have a small piano, a bean bag chair, a talking dog that speaks in Spanish, English and French, and all kinds of things that promise to keep drawers and cabinets safely locked. I never knew there was so much to worry about with little ones, or that there were so many dangers within my home.

Pushing the heavy cart toward the checkout lanes, I'm struck with a thought. Collins encouraged me to fight for her, but what if Elan is doing this same thing right now? Not knowing what I'm up against makes me feel edgy. I know in my heart that I'm the better man for her. I would never leave her scared and alone to deal with the after effects of our actions. He's already left her once. Who's to say he won't do it again when things get tough?

I stop at the checkout counter and the young cashier beams up at me. "Wow. Stocking up, huh?"

"Yeah, something like that." Even I have to admit, it's probably a little odd to head out in the middle of the night and buy pretty much one of everything at a superstore in the suburbs. But Kylie inspired something inside of me. I feel different than I've ever felt before, and I am going to fight for her.

After unloading my car and bringing all the baby stuff inside and setting it up, it's nearly four in the morning. Time for some sleep. Tomorrow will be a big day.

KYLIE

I tossed and turned all night, so when Max wakes up crying at six in the morning, I'm groggy and exhausted. I lift him one-armed from his crib and change his soaking wet diaper. His newest discovery seems to be his penis. *Oh, joy.* Every time I take his diaper off, he reaches down for it and tugs and pulls, in what seems like it'd be a painful way, but he doesn't seem bothered.

It only reminds me that I'm raising a boy —complete with all the parts and workings of a boy. He is going to need a man in his life. Sure, I can have the birds and the bees talk with him, but I'm fully aware that he would benefit from a man's perspective. Someone to discuss sports, and women with. I picture myself muttering, *Go ask your dad*, and smile. Until I realize it's not Elan in my mind's eye. It's Pace.

The smile falls from my mouth and I shake the thoughts away.

After Max is dressed and is quietly eating breakfast in his highchair, I make an extra strong cup of coffee and grab my phone.

I find a text from Pace sent at three in the morning. Wow, late night. I find myself wondering who he was out with, and what he was doing. *It's not my business.* His text is straight to the point.

I need to talk to you today.

I owe him that much at least. He's been so kind and generous with me and Max. I kind of just stormed into his life, and then out of it. Not that I would think a man like him would mind. I shrug away the sullen thoughts and hit reply.

Sure. What did you have in mind?

Can you guys come by later? Stay for dinner?

I take a deep breathe. I want to reply, *Yes, yes, yes!* But I temper my longing for a man that was never really mine to begin with. I need to think about what is best for my son. I glance over at Max. Knowing how much he enjoys being near Pace, and also that I owe Pace an explanation in person, I decide maybe we should go.

I will be there.

A text message pings a few minutes later, and a silly smile graces my lips. I assume it's Pace replying. But it's Elan.

How are you and my son on this fine morning?

My stomach churns. I glance over at Max who's happily eating chunks of bananas and dry cereal.

We're fine, thanks.

It's strange to think I dated this man for six months, that we have a child together, and yet I feel like I have nothing to say to him. I suppose it's because we haven't spoken for so long. There's bound to be some awkward silences as we reacquaint with one another.

What are you doing this weekend? I would like to see you again.

I chew on my lip.

Sure. We don't have any plans.

Okay, I will call you Saturday morning. We can meet for brunch.

I don't tell him that Max usually takes a nap late-morning, or that a restaurant might not be the best place to meet. I don't want to crush whatever this is building between us. He will learn how to be a father, and I will help him.

***

I tote Max on my hip with the diaper bag slung over my arm. This whole doing everything one-handed business is already getting old. And I have a long ways to go before my cast will be removed. I take a deep breath and try to calm my nerves.

"We're going to see Pace," I tell Max as we head upstairs toward Pace's condo.

"Pa-pa," he says, clapping his chubby hands.

"Pace," I correct him, my voice coming out more firm than I intended.

Pace opens the door before I even have a chance to knock. He must have been watching for us.

"Hi," I say.

"Hi." His eyes are guarded and I wonder how tonight is going to go. He takes Max from me, lifting him into his arms and tossing him up in the air to coax a laugh from him. "Hey buddy, you remember me?" he asks.

"Pa-pa," Max murmurs.

"That's right. Papa Pace." Pace beams at him and my stomach twists.

We step inside and a few things hit me at once. The scent of appetizing food wafts from the kitchen and I notice new toys are scattered on the living room rug. "Pace?" I ask.

He doesn't answer right away, he just carries Max into the living room and sets him down amongst the pile of toys.

I follow them, my heart beating fast. "What is all this?"

Pace sinks down to his knees and watches Max go after an inflatable bouncy dragon. He chuckles. "I knew you'd like him," he says. Then he turns to me, his smile faltering just a bit. "This is me showing you that I am in this. I am not giving up on you, or on Max. If Elan's back in Max's life – fine. But I'm not going anywhere."

My heart kicks in my chest as his words tug at me. I look around at the pile of new playthings, there are books and age appropriate toys and things for learning. Tears spring to my eyes. His thoughtfulness shouldn't surprise me at this point, but no one has ever done something so sweet and meaningful before. "What did you do?" I whisper, taking it all in.

"I wanted Max to be comfortable here. I also wanted you to be comfortable, so in addition to the toys, I did some baby-proofing. The cabinets now have safety locks and the outlets all have covers."

I glance around his condo and notice the little plastic covers have been inserted into all the wall outlets and the potted palm in the dining room that Max liked to dig in is no longer resting in its spot in the corner. I swallow down the lump rising in my throat. His gestures are too much.

"Excuse me for a minute," I squeak and head into the bathroom, drawing deep pulls of oxygen into my lungs as I lock the door behind me. *Who is this man? What happened to the cocky, smart-mouthed player? This man is gentle and kind and... my heart feels like it's breaking in two.*

I want to sneak a phone call to Rachel, to ask her what she thinks all of this means. *Has he changed? Am I the exception to the rule?* Knowing I can't hide in the bathroom, as much as I might want to, I splash cool water on my cheeks and check my reflection in the mirror. My green eyes are watery and my cheeks are flushed. I don't want to appear as though I've been crying. That will only inspire questions from Pace I can't answer.

After I've composed myself, I meet Pace and Max in the living room. They're sitting on the floor surrounded by a mountain of toys, happily talking away in the language that only they seem to know.

"Everything okay?" Pace glances up at me, looking solemn.

I nod. "Everything's fine," I confirm. My hands are trembling, but I sink to the floor beside Max, trying my damnedest to pretend like Pace didn't just rock my entire world.

"How did things go with Elan after I left yesterday?" he asks.

His eyes might be on the set of colorful blocks he's stacking with Max, but his question has all kinds of weight to it, and his voice is rich with emotion.

"It's going to take some time," I say. "But I think it was a good start. He couldn't believe how much Max looks like him."

Pace nods, his eyes downcast on the tower he and Max are building. "It'll be good for Max, I'm sure. Having his biological father in his life."

I nod in agreement.

Pace lifts his head, his gorgeous deep blue eyes meeting mine. "And what about you? Where do you and Elan stand?"

I swallow a sudden wave of nerves that dance in my belly. "I-I don't know," I admit. "He wants me back," I add, softly.

"I see," Pace bites out in a clipped tone.

We sit in silence for several moments and watch Max drive trucks all over the carpeting and crash them into the legs of Pace's couch.

Thankfully, Max has no idea about the tension that exists between us. I can't believe that just two nights ago Pace and I had hot, frantic sex on the desk in his office and now it feels like there is an ocean of distance between us.

"Are you guy's hungry?" Pace asks finally.

I make the sign for *eat* to Max, and he does repeats it eagerly, bringing his hand to his mouth and mimicking me. Pace and I both laugh. "I guess that's a yes."

P*ACE*

I remove the casserole dish from the oven while Kylie gets Max settled in the new booster seat I bought for the dining room table. I thought about buying a high chair, but the sales clerk insisted this seat with its safety harness would be fine for a one-year old. It seems like it is, and plus now Max can eat at the table with us. Although the voice inside of me points out that this could be the last time they're over for dinner.

Pushing the dark thoughts aside, I dish up servings of the homemade macaroni and cheese that I once made for Sophie after the death of her sister. Comfort food. It smells great and looks like it turned out well too.

"Wow. Is that homemade?" Kylie asks, peeking over my shoulder as I spoon out a small serving for Max onto a plastic plate. Another of my new purchases. Along with little plastic spoons and sippy cups. Dear God, this has to work. Or I will be left with an entire home of baby items that I don't need. I'd wanted to get a crib too, and move my office furniture from the guest room to outfit it for Max. I even browsed through a baby furniture catalog at the store last night, but when I realized that if Kylie chooses Elan, I couldn't handle walking past a nursery every day. It would be a constant reminder that I'd lost them.

"Yes," I answer stiffly. "It's homemade."

"It looks great." Kylie smiles brightly up at me, and I decide I have no idea how to read her. She seemed angry and detached when she first got here, and now she seems happy to be here with me.

We eat dinner, making occasional small talk, and we mostly watch Max. To say he's enthusiastic about the macaroni would be an understatement. By the end of the meal, I'm pretty sure he's not only covered in it, he's smeared it into his hair and eyebrows.

"The offer still stands for you to use the hose out back to rinse him off," I joke.

She shakes her head. "Actually, could I use your bathtub again? There's no way I'm putting him in my car like this."

"Of course. I'll start the water if you like."

"Okay."

Once again, we leave the dishes abandoned on the table and head into the master bath with a squirming, filthy toddler between us. I feel a routine developing, but then again, I can't get my hopes up. She could choose Elan, and all of this would be taken from me. It's not a thought I want to dwell on.

Kylie strips him down to his diaper right there on the bathroom floor, while I fill the tub, making sure the water isn't too hot.

While we bath him together, my eyes keep wandering over to hers. I want to know what she's thinking. I want to know where we stand.

A strange sensation washes over me. I want to bare my soul to her, and beg her not to leave. Christ, is this what Colton felt like on the verge of losing Sophie? The feeling is terrifying. It's free-falling with no net, it's like being on a roller coaster with no safety harness. No wonder Colt flew coach all the way to Italy when she left. I would cross any mountain, tear down any barrier for a chance to make her mine.

When I catch her watching me too, I decide to take a chance.

"I thought the other night meant something," I say. "It did for me. I know how rare that was for you, and I want you to know it was for me too." I didn't bring women home and I sure as hell didn't fuck them bareback.

Kylie's eyes find mine, while her hand rests on Max's shoulder. While he sits pretty well in the tub, he's still unpredictable and squirmy. "I thought it was too. It was one of the best nights of my life, but when you left the morning after without saying anything – without even a goodbye kiss, I'd assumed that I imagined the whole thing. I figured I'd imagined the intimacy we shared, the closeness I felt was all just in my head because I wanted it to be there. I wanted to believe you were a reformed playboy."

"Who I was before became irrelevant the moment I met you. None of those women were worth settling down for."

"And me and Max…we're worth it?"

"Most definitely. I would keep you both permanently if I could."

She opens her mouth like she wants to argue, but she doesn't. She suddenly closes it and stares straight at me. "Is that what all this baby-proofing was about?"

"Yes. I meant what I said. I want you both to be happy here."

"I am happy, but…"

"But," I repeat and give her a playful look. I know she's about to interject with something about Elan. "No buts, just for tonight. Let's pretend it's me, and you, and Max, and no one else."

"Okay," she whispers.

After Max is washed from head to toe, Kylie grabs the towel.

"Let me," I tell her. Fishing him from the tub, I carefully lift his wet, slippery little body, knowing I'm holding something very precious.

After Max is dried and in a fresh diaper, I dress him in one of my T-shirts. The thing falls to his ankles and he thinks it's hilarious. Kylie does too, they both openly giggle and dance around my bedroom. My home has never been filled with this much laughter. This much love. It stops me in my tracks. I just stand there, holding a wet towel, soaking it all in.

Max heads to the bed, and grabs fistfuls of the duvet cover and begins pulling himself up onto the bed.

"Mumma." He pats the bed bedside him. "Pa-pa," he says patting the other side.

His innocent gesture means so much more, but of course he has no way of knowing that.

"It looks like he wants to stay the night again," I say, watching for Kylie's reaction. Obviously nothing would make me happier. "What do you say?" The promise of another intimate encounter dances delicately between us. The hungry look in her eyes gives away her desire. "Say yes," I tell her.

"Yes," she breathes.

We settle on either side of Max, as he instructed, and I lift the copy of *Goodnight Moon* from the shelf beside my bed. I hand the book to Kylie, but she shakes her head.

"No, you read it tonight."

I open to the first page and begin, wondering how long it's been since I last read a children's book.

KYLIE

Pace's masculine voice reading *Goodnight Moon* puts me in a happy little place of bliss. One where there are no thoughts of custody arrangements looming over me, or the pull of two very different men, for two very different reasons.

Max is evidently in his happy place too. His eyes are big and he listens attentively, staying as quiet and still as a little mouse.

I don't think he's ever had a man read to him before, and there is something distinctly different about the entire experience. In addition to his rich, deep tone caressing the words, Pace lingers over different parts of the story, points out objects on the page and names them, pauses at the turn of each new page so they can admire the illustration. It's a magical thing watching them read together. If what Pace said was genuine, we could have this every night. The thought is intoxicating.

After Max is asleep, we clean the dishes together in silence. I sense we're both processing the weight of everything that's happened between us.

Sometimes I wish I was a normal girl, to which the normal rules of dating applied – dinner and a movie and a kiss on my front porch. It seems so much easier, so much less confusing, without all the complications of my family obligations and responsibilities. But of course, I wouldn't trade Max for anything in the world, so that's out.

"How's your arm?" Pace asks out of the blue.

"Still sore, but I'm managing." I feel like I can be honest with him, even if I don't want to totally admit to my weakness.

"We're just about done here, why don't you go relax in the living room?" he says. "I'll finish up here, grab a beer, and then join you."

"Okay." I know better than to try and argue.

Pace's living room is still destroyed with toys scattered everywhere, so while I wait for him, I pick up every last toy, one at a time and line them up in a neat pile along the wall. It seems the only item he forgot was a toy box to house all these new treasures.

When Pace wanders in a few minutes later with a bottle of imported beer dangling in one hand, he takes a brief look around and shakes his head at me. That delectable smirk and dimpled grin makes me weak in the knees. Good thing I'm already seated.

I know he knows the effect he can have on a woman when he's working his game, but I don't think he has any idea how deeply he can affect me without even trying. Just the sight of him provokes a physical response in my body. My belly is a mess of nerves, my palms begin shaking and my breasts feel so sensitive, they're tingling for his mouth again. I'm terrified Pace can see right through me when he looks at me like that – all intense and brooding. But the next words out of his mouth ease my mind. He doesn't know I have sex on the brain.

"Do you even know how to relax?" he asks.

I don't respond. I'm a single mom who works full-time. My opportunities for lounging and eating bon-bons are limited to say the least.

He chuckles, his mood suddenly turning light. "Come here." He sits down on the couch and pats the cushion beside him. I slide closer, wondering what type of relaxation he has in mind. Something of the orgasmic variety, I hope. I want to bitch-slap my subconscious. *No. Definitely no.*

Pace places his hands at my waist and turns my body so I'm angled away from him. I'm reminded instantly how powerful and strong he is, remembering how he so easily lifted me onto the desk when we made love. A thrill of excitement races through me. I recall the exquisite feeling of his wicked hands on my skin, his lips at my throat, his powerful cock sliding in and out of me. Everything had been perfect, but I couldn't allow myself to think about that now. Not when Elan was seemingly back in the picture. Pushing those thoughts from my head, I focus on Pace's large hands on my shoulders. He gives them a squeeze, and I swear my muscles go instantly lax.

Ohhh.

"You're so tense," he murmurs, rubbing his thumbs along my shoulder blades.

His hands are magic as he rubs my shoulders with firm pressure and I feel my body relaxing into the sofa. But when he starts massaging the back of my neck, his fingers pressing into my scalp, I completely lose my composure, whimpering and leaning into his touch.

"That's it, let me take care of you," he whispers, his fingers lightly massaging, and caressing. I close my eyes and just enjoy the sensations. Everything in my life feels so confusing, and so heavy, but in this moment, I let myself enjoy the stillness of the moment. I deserve this much.

When Pace finishes the massage, I'm lax and almost boneless. I could curl into him and fall asleep. He turns me to face him and meets my eyes, while running his fingers through the long strands of my hair. "How did that feel?" he asks, his voice quiet.

"Really good," I admit. "Thank you. For dinner, for the toys, for everything..." He is too much, his kindness shines through with every action. My own words float through my head. I'd once told Pace that the quality I was looking for in a man is someone who was kind to my child. But he's shown me something even more – he's amazing with Max, but he's also there for *me*. My throat gets tight.

"You're welcome." His voice is hoarse, and suddenly I realize he's aroused. I glance down and see a bulge pressing against his trousers. Touching me, even in an innocent fashion, has turned him on. Remembering that he doesn't wear boxers makes me realize if I were to unzip the front of his pants, I could have his hot length in my greedy hands.

Feeling bold, I settle my hand over the front of his pants, lightly palming his erection.

A strangled groan pushes past his lips and his eyes land on mine. "Kylie..." His voice is a tender plea in the silent room, and the coarse quality to it sends shivers along my body. He wants me. And, even if it's just for tonight, I want to feel wanted.

Sinking to the floor between his feet, my shaky hands fumble with his button and zipper while my eyes stay on his. I'm too filled with my need for him to worry about the consequences of Max finding us.

Pace's breathing increases and his hand cups my cheek, his thumb lightly dancing along my skin.

I don't know what I'm doing, but I know that I want my mouth on him. I want to give back all the pleasure he's given to me. I want to make him feel as helpless and out of control as I do.

Once his pants are open and his big, beautiful cock is in my hand, I lower my mouth to the tip, and open wide, trying to fit my mouth around him. I inadvertently make a sucking sound against him and Pace groans out a curse word.

"Fuck." His hands push into my hair and I think he's going to take control, to push himself deep into my throat and fuck my mouth, but he only massages my scalp and plays with my hair while I continue working him over. I sweep my tongue across the head of him and tease him with broad licks of my tongue before lowering my mouth all the way down his shaft. His hands still and he groans. "That feels so good," he encourages when I ease up and slid down again. His hands stay buried in my hair while I bob up and down his length, eagerly sucking him.

He moves his hands move from my hair, and places one palm against my cheek. I open my eyes and look up at him. The smoldering look in his eyes makes my panties wet. He's so utterly strong and sexy, and his cock is buried in my mouth.

"Goddamn, you're so good at this," he moans.

He's pulsing and wet with my saliva, and I slip my hand up and down over his steely length. Pace wraps his hand around mine, showing me that he likes a firmer grip and chokes out a groan when I tighten my hand on him. "That's it."

His eyes stay on mine while my hand pumps up and down. My tongue licks at the tip of him, tasting the drop of liquid that appears.

"If you don't want me to come, you need to stop now," he warns.

Of course I want him to. I continue my slow, wet kisses to the head while my hand slides up and down.

A rich rumble erupts in his chest and his hand grips mine once again, stilling my movements. I close my mouth around him as hot jets of semen slide down my throat. He is so perfect, so masculine and sexy, and geez, he even tastes good. I swallow every bit of him while he growls out another curse and his hand involuntarily tightens in my hair.

I wipe my lips with the back of my hand and glance up at him.

He's smiling his gorgeous crooked smile that shows off his dimple. "I don't know what I did to deserve that, but shit, that was good. Come here." He takes my hand and pulls me up into his lap.

I can't help the girly giggle that rises from my throat. Being near him, letting go, it all just makes me feel so light and carefree.

Moments like this are rare for me, and I want to savor this feeling, to bottle it up.

Pace, not seeming to mind in the least that his semen was just in my mouth, brings his lips to mine and kisses me, gently at first, then with a heated passion that makes my toes curl.

His hands slide under my shirt and his thumbs graze my nipples. I shiver at the pleasurable contact. It's exactly what I've been craving. He's always so sure and confident with his movements, it makes me love the commanding, masculine side to him. His hands move around to my back, where he quickly unclasps my bra, and then his hands are once again at my breasts, massaging them and stroking my tight nipples.

"I love your chest," he whispers, burying his face against my neck and lightly kissing. My head falls back, giving him access to my throat. I love the feel of his mouth on me. I squirm in his lap, my wet panties clinging to my sensitive flesh, as he caresses my breasts.

"Pace," I groan.

I feel him begin to harden beneath me and a surprised gasp leaves my throat. "Again?" I ask, unable to hide my shock that he can be hard again so quickly.

He shrugs. "I'm twenty-five, babe. I can come two or three times before I need a break." His smile is cocky and sure, but I guess it's not cocky if it's true.

Dear God, this information wreaks havoc on my libido. Any man who has that type of control over his body is just freaking sexy.

He pushes his hips up and grinds his erect cock into me. "Are you wet for me?" he asks, his tone direct.

My inner muscles clench in excitement. "Y-yes," I stammer. I'm unsure why but he's turned me into a complete wanton mess.

"Can I make love to you right here on the couch?" he asks.

My eyes dart to the bedroom door. Max never wakes once he's down for the night. My gaze returns to Pace's and his navy eyes burn hotly on mine. "Yes," I say.

He pulls my shirt off over my head and his mouth lowers to my right breast, sucking my nipple into the hot cavern of his mouth and licking his tongue over it again and again. I toss my head back and groan, and Pace moves to the other breast, treating it to the same pleasure.

"Stand up, baby."

I rise off his lap and stand in front of him. Pace's jeans are still pushed down his hips and his heavy cock is resting against his belly. It is a beautiful sight. His fingers reach for the button on my jeans and once he undoes it and tugs down my zipper, I help him push my jeans and underwear down my hips. I step out of them, and then I'm back in his lap.

Pace grips his erection, his hand sliding up and down lazily over his shaft while my eyes grow wide watching him. I love watching him touch himself. The way he tugs on his thick cock, while his eyes are glazed over with lust is incredibly sexy. I feel like I'm being treated to a private erotic show.

"Lower yourself down on me," he says, keeping one hand on his base and the other at my hip.

I angle myself over the top of him and feel him nudge at my wet center. We both groan at the warm contact as our bodies come together. He thrusts his hips up at the same time that I push mine down, and I have to bite into my lower lip to keep from screaming out. He is large, but he fills me perfectly. I sink lower, rotating my hips to take him deep. *Dear, God.*

His eyes slide closed and his head falls back against the couch. "Fuck."

I love that I just made him lose control and come in my mouth not even five minutes ago and he's already overwhelmed with pleasure once again.

Gripping my hips in both hands, Pace thrusts up, stilling once he's fully buried inside me. His blue eyes find mine and his look is so tender and loving, it makes my heart ache. He can't look at me like that. I close my eyes, and begin to move, bouncing on his thick erection, up and down, so that with each stroke, he's massaging that pleasurable spot deep inside. I am so aroused, I know it's not going to take me long to come.

We move together, completely in sync, just like the last time, and while our mouths stay fused together in a deep, passionate kiss, our bodies work in tandem to achieve the maximum amount of pleasure we can derive. Sex has never felt so good. And I'm certain the difference is Pace. The depth of my feelings for him scare me, but there is no denying our connection. Watching him build a slow relationship with both me and my child has allowed us to connect on a deeper level, and that intense connection has obviously translated into the bedroom – or living room, as it were.

"That's it, baby." Pace's big hand curls around my hip, guiding my movements. "Ride it like you own it," he says, bringing his mouth to mine.

His words pull at something inside me. I know in that moment that I do own a piece of his heart and I put everything I have, everything I am into this moment, tightening my inner muscles around him and riding him with reckless abandon.

PACE

Kylie tightens her muscles around my cock and a strangled groan rises up my throat. Watching her move on top of me is incredibly erotic. In this moment she is free. Free from everything – all the worry and stress in her life – and I love that I not only get to share this moment with her, but that I am the one to take her there.

"Can you come again?" I ask her. Her first orgasm was explosive – she trembled in my arms and cried out my name again and again.

"I don't know," she says.

"It might take me a little while to get there," I admit.

A slow smile uncurls on her mouth. She likes this. Good.

I spend the next fifteen minutes teasing two more orgasms from her. I hunt out all of her sensitive spots – her nipples and clit, obviously, but also discover the spot behind her knee and the dip in her throat that also make her squirm. I know I've pushed her to her limits when her eyes glaze over with exhaustion and her body is covered in a damp sheen of sweat. I pick up my pace, fucking her hard and fast, thrusting up into her tight warmth that fits me like a glove.

My balls tighten against my body just as I'm overcome with a powerful release. I bury my face against her throat and grip her ass in both hands as I release inside of her warm body.

After, she curls into me and I wrap my arms around her and just hold her to my chest, my softening cock still inside her. This moment means something. I know she can feel it just like I can, but I also know she has a bad habit of pushing me away.

I hold her close, loving the feel of her head against my chest. I kiss the top of her head and tell her how amazing that was. She makes a little noise of agreement, but doesn't move from the warm spot she's claimed. It's only when her breathing slows and her body goes completely lax in my arms that I realize she's fallen asleep. I chuckle to myself, rather enjoying the fact that I worked her over so completely she's passed out on top of me – with my cock still inside of her.

Careful not to wake her, I lay her down on the couch, gathering a handful of tissues to wipe between her legs where the after-effect of my orgasm is beginning to show. Seeing my come decorating her delicate pink folds makes me half hard again. But we've both had multiple orgasms in the last hour, so I will let her sleep. She murmurs something as she feels me clean between her legs, but her eyes stay closed. It's like she's been drugged. I smile proudly.

Once she's clean, I dress Kylie in her t-shirt, and then slide her panties up her legs. She curls onto her side on the couch, cradling her casted arm close to her body, and I join her, pulling a blanket over us and tucking her body in close to mine. I'd never fully appreciated spooning until this moment. With my body curled around hers, I close my eyes and let myself drift off into that relaxed state just before sleep takes over.

"Goodnight, Moon," I whisper with my lips pressed to her hair, thankful that even if it's just for tonight, she's in my arms.

***

At some point in the night, she had gone. Left me alone on the couch in favor of Max. Something unsettled me about that, as if it was a metaphor for our entire relationship. She was too scared to feel something for me, and rather than staying with me and taking the risk, she'd gone back to the safety and comfort of what she knew. A sense of loss greater than I'd ever known fills me.

Stiff, and still groggy, I sit up and stretch my arms over my head. Images of last night's intense sexual encounter dance through my brain, warming me.

As I make coffee in the kitchen, I hear voices from inside my bedroom. I listen more closely and smile at the soft notes of her singing baby songs to Max. My heart speeds up, knowing it's Saturday and that I have the entire day to look forward to with them.

I rummage through the fridge and cabinets in search of something to make them for breakfast. Just as I settle on eggs and toast, Kylie comes out of the bedroom carrying Max. He is still dressed in my t-shirt, and for some reason that makes me smile. Kylie is dressed in the same clothes as yesterday and her hair is tied back in a low ponytail.

"Morning," I say, leaning in to kiss her cheek.

She pulls back suddenly, her eyes betraying her confusion.

"Everything okay?" I ask, sensing an unwelcome shift between us.

"Yes, everything's fine," she says. "I just can't believe we stayed the night. I don't have any more diapers and of course Max is completely soaked."

I'm intuitive enough to know it's not the lack of diapers that has her frazzled, but I won't pry right now. Something tells me if I do, I'll only push her away. "I don't suppose some paper towels and duct tape would work?" I ask, giving her a grin.

She laughs. "No, I don't think so, but that's very MacGyver of you."

"I can run to the store while you guys have breakfast. The eggs are ready." I glance toward the cook top where the skillet of scrambled eggs waits.

"No, that's sweet of you, but we need to get home."

I swallow an uncomfortable lump in my throat. "I was hoping you would stay, spend the day here. We could take a walk down to the park."

She chews on her lower lip like she has something unpleasant to tell me. "We're meeting Elan for brunch later this morning."

My hands curl into fists, but I don't respond.

"I thought I explained this to you. I thought you understood that Elan and I have a history and we're…"

I hold up a hand, stopping her. "It's fine. I understand that you have a history with him. You have a baby for fucks sake." Kylie cringes at my rough tone. "I'm sorry." Shit, why can't I do anything right? Why can't I get this woman to see how much I care about her? It's fucking infuriating. And after the night we just shared, I thought we were past this. I don't spoon with women after sex or gently wipe them clean. Kylie is the exception to everything.

Awkwardly, she turns away from me and I see her wipe her eyes.

Dammit.

Then she grabs her purse from the back of the chair and slings it over her body. "I guess we're gonna go," she says.

"Pa-pa," Max says, reaching for me.

"Have fun with your dad, buddy," I tell him, my voice sounding oddly cold and disengaged. I want to take him in my arms and hug his little body to mine, but I don't. It will only hurt worse.

I know I should offer to walk her out, help her get Max into the car. But I don't. Instead, I grab a plate from the counter and begin piling eggs on it.

"Bye Pace," Kylie whispers. I don't turn toward her. I don't want her to see the tears swimming in my eyes.

I hear the door click closed and I hurl the plate against the wall, the porcelain shattering and eggs flying everywhere.

"Fuck!" I roar.

The empty, too-quiet condo feels cold and hollow.

I sink to my knees on the kitchen floor, and begin picking up pieces of broken glass. If I can't win her over with my actions, or my words, I'm lost. I gave her everything I had last night. I bared myself. My feelings for her and for Max were right there at the surface. Today, I feel raw and broken, like a piece of me is missing. She saw me – the true me, and everything I had to offer as a man, a lover and as a father, and still, she's chosen to walk away – chosen him. Elan might share Max's DNA, but he hasn't given them a piece of his heart like I have.

Chapter Thirteen

Elan sits across the table from me, sipping his coffee and quietly watching Max. The restaurant is more upscale than I would have preferred. I'm not opposed to taking Max out to eat, but generally choose somewhere loud and kid-friendly. This quiet, quaint bistro is neither. In fact, I think Max is the only child in the place. Thankfully, the restaurant did have a highchair when I asked for one, and Max is seated in between Elan and I, happily munching on crackers that I've broken up in front of him. The dirty scowls from the waitress tells me that she's definitely noticed the pile of crumbs he's creating on the floor.

"What did you guys do last night?" Elan asks, breaking my concentration.

"Us?" I squeak out. "Nothing. I mean, we ate dinner and then Max had a bath." *Oh, and then got my brains fucked out by a man I think I'm falling in love with.*

He nods.

The waitress comes by and we order our food, Belgian waffles for me and Max, and poached eggs for Elan. I feel terribly guilty about the way I left Pace this morning. The smell of scrambled eggs and toast coming from the kitchen, coupled with the sight of a rumpled, sleepy Pace were hard to resist. But Elan is Max's father, I have to see if this could work, right?

As I watch Elan and Max, I'm struck by a sinking feeling. They may look alike, but that's where the similarities end. Max is eager and friendly, and babbles nonstop. Elan is composed and calculated, and a man of few words.

Elan seems cold and distant. I realize with trepidation these are not qualities I want my son to learn. But Max doesn't seem all that interested in Elan. I remember how even in the beginning, he went right to Pace. Of course Pace, so confident and open, smiled and talked to him. Elan is doing none of those things.

"I wanted to bring him a toy, but I didn't know what to get that might be age-appropriate," Elan says after several minutes of awkward silence.

That never stopped Pace. Again, I'm with Elan and all I can think about is Pace and how the man in front of me doesn't measure up. I can't help but recall the tender, yet intense way he made love to me last night. His fingers curling into my hips and his teeth lightly grazing my lower lip.

Elan walked out on me, believing that chasing his own happiness did not involve me or a baby. I am self-aware enough to know that my happiness centers on a sticky, nonsense-babbling tiny person. Elan was a fool not to see that. Not to even step foot onto this adventure. And it's too late now. And while I know that being a parent isn't easy, Pace isn't just willing to take it on. He's practically begging for the chance.

Suddenly, I feel like I can't breathe. I know I've made a terrible mistake pushing him away in favor of Elan – the man who'd left me when I'd been at my most vulnerable. Pace had been my knight – coming to my rescue when I needed it most.

I rise from the table. "I'm sorry. I thought I could do this, but I can't. If you want visitation, we can work that out. But you and I…" I pause, drawing a deep breath. "We are through. The day I told you I was pregnant, and you left, that is not something that I can overcome. I want a man who sees my worth, and not someone who's willing to take me back despite what he sees as a flaw."

"Kylie, I…"

"No." My tone is resolute.

His mouth closes. He can tell that I'm done. He folds his hands in front of him while his expression remains cool and neutral. He is not even going to fight for me. For his son. No, this is not a man that I want Max to grow up idolizing and imitating.

I swallow down a lump of sadness and lift Max from the highchair. "Text me, and we can arrange for visitation." And with that, I stride to the exit and toward what I hope is my future.

***

When I arrive back at Pace's condo, there is no answer at the door. I twist the knob and find it unlocked, so I let myself in.

"Pace?" I call out, adjusting Max on my hip.

No response.

I step further into his home, finding the kitchen and living room both empty. I'd been so frantic to get back here, but now it seems he's not even home.

I hear a sound coming from his bedroom.

A woman's giggle.

My stomach plummets, and I feel a wave of nausea rise up my throat.

Oh, dear God, I'm too late. He has a woman here. I need to shield Max from whatever I'm certain is happening in that bedroom, so I set him down in the living room with the pile of toys. But I have to see with my own eyes. It is the only thing that will break this spell Pace has over me.

I tiptoe toward his room. I can hear the woman say something, but I don't hear Pace respond. A quick glance back at Max shows me that he's playing happily. With my stomach twisted into a painful knot, my feet carry me toward Pace's room.

The bedroom door is closed, and once again the soft hush of feminine laughter sounds from within. The laughter seems so out of place when all I feel like doing is crying. But if she's laughing rather than moaning, maybe I've caught him before he's completely indisposed.

Swallowing down my fears, along with my pride, I raise my uninjured hand and knock on the door.

"Pace? I need to speak with you," I say in the calmest voice I can manage when my heart is slamming against my ribcage.

There's no response.

I raise my hand to knock again when the door suddenly opens.

"Kylie?" Pace's confusion lines his face. For once his expression is cold and serious. Gone is the playful, easy to get along with man I've fallen for.

He's fully dressed, and I peer around him into the bedroom – which appears to be empty. The copy of *Goodnight Moon* is still sitting on his nightstand. I feel heartbroken just looking at it. I'll never be able to read it again without thinking of him and all that I lost.

"What are you doing here?" he asks.

"Where is she?"

"Who?" he says.

"I heard a woman, Pace. Don't try and deny it."

His expression turns from confused to angry, his mouth drawing into a firm line. "You just refuse to see the real me, is that it? You're so utterly convinced I'm still that irresponsible guy on the prowl that you refuse to believe I might be looking for something real."

"Pace, I heard her," I say, standing my ground, even though his words have pierced the very center of me. He doesn't respond so I storm past him, and look around the room, searching out the bathroom and his large walk-in closet as well. The room is empty. Well, that's not entirely true, because upon hearing our voices, Max has wandered in and is now in Pace's arms.

Pace grabs the remote control from the bed and presses a button. The TV screen comes to life, displaying a man and a woman.

"I was watching a movie," he says.

When the woman laughs, I realize that is the sound I heard.

My relief is instant, and sobering. "I'm sorry," I say.

"For not believing in me or for leaving?" he asks.

"For everything." I sink down onto the edge of his bed, my heart feeling heavy. The adrenaline surge I felt just moments ago, thinking I was about to discover him in a sordid act, makes my pulse plummet. I feel drained. "I was scared, Pace. Scared of feeling something real for you. Scared you couldn't possibly return those feelings."

"This is as real as it gets, angel," he says.

"I know that now."

"So what happened with you and Elan?" he asks, his voice guarded.

"If Elan wants a relationship with Max, I won't keep him from that. But I have no interest in him, not romantically, anyway." I glance up at Pace, unsure of what he's thinking. He's never normally so guarded. "If you'll still have me..." I start.

Pace steps closer and reaches for my hand. I place my palm against his and he pulls me up so I'm standing before him. "I'm keeping you for always. I thought I told you that."

He leans in, and with Max still in his arms, he kisses me right on the mouth. I kiss him back, my heart thumping wildly. I'm sure he understands that he's the first man I've let kiss me in front of my son.

"You're stubborn as hell, you know that, right?" Pace asks, pulling back with a smile hot enough to singe.

"What makes you say that?"

"You fought my every advance. I've never worked this hard in my damn life."

I laugh softly. "I did put up one hell of a fight, but you're a hard man to resist," I admit.

"Did something happen this morning? Did Elan do something to change your mind?"

"No. It was all the things he didn't do. He doesn't connect with Max like you do. He doesn't make me feel safe and secure. And he certainly doesn't make me feel out of control with desire."

"Out of control?" he asks, his voice dropping lower. "Last night was…incredible," he admits, planting a kiss on my forehead.

"Yes, it was," I agree. I'd never felt so deeply connected to a man when he was inside of me like I did with Pace. Sex was just sex, but with him, it was something else entirely. It was so much more. I could lose control and let go, something I rarely did in my day-to-day life. The sensation was freeing.

I had no idea what would happen next, and as it turned out, Pace proved to be anything but an ordinary boyfriend.

Chapter Fourteen

It feels so good to finally have my arm out of the cast. I stretch my arms leisurely above my head, wincing at the small ache when I bend my elbow. I study myself in the full length mirror in my bedroom, and smooth my black sleeveless dress over my hips. My poor arm looks pale and scrawny. I add several long layering necklaces, hoping the bling will draw the attention away from my arm. I have no idea what we're doing tonight. Pace said to be ready at six o'clock, and when I'd asked about Max, he just smiled and said he had everything covered. I wasn't sure what his vague answer meant, so I'd probed my nanny for details. I'd asked if she was staying late tonight and watching him, she'd merely smiled and said that she'd been sworn to secrecy. Then she added that I shouldn't worry, and yes, she was taking care of Max tonight.

I hadn't been on a proper date in forever, and Pace and I had never actually been on a real date, sans baby, since we started dating six weeks ago. I was almost giddy at the thought of being alone with him. I hoped I could control myself long enough at a restaurant, because I was majorly looking forward to being alone with him. Alone, alone.

Glancing at the clock, I see it's just now six, so I step into my black heels and grab my miniature handbag. Carrying this thing is a treat – normally my extra-large purse also housed pacifiers, diapers and baby toys.

I hear voices from the living room and when I enter, Pace is standing talking to my nanny, Lynn. They both fall silent as I enter the room.

"What's with all the secrecy?" I ask, grinning at my adorably sexy boyfriend.

He treats me to a crooked grin and drags his eyes down my body. "You look stunning."

"Thank you," I murmur, my cheeks suddenly heating. I take a moment to admire him as well. Pace is dressed smartly in tailored black pants, and a white dress shirt with a black tie knotted loosely at his neck. His shirtsleeves are rolled up several times, exposing strong, tanned forearms. He looks delicious. Good enough to eat. And suddenly, I'm starving, but it's not for dinner.

"We better get going, we've got a schedule to maintain," Pace says.

I nod, then turn to Lynn, who is holding Max on her hip. "Are you sure you guys will be okay? I have a leftover chicken casserole in the fridge for dinner, and…"

She stops me with a dismissive wave of her hand. "We will be just fine, Kylie. You deserve a night out. Enjoy it."

I nod. Lynn is amazing, and Max loves spending time with her. I know I have nothing to worry about. "Thank you."

Pace offers me his arm and he leads me outside, where there is a black stretch limousine waiting for us at the curb. A slow smile uncurls on my mouth. "Well, this is unexpected," I say.

"We're going to have fun tonight," he says, fighting off a grin of his own.

I know Pace is wealthy, but he doesn't throw his money around or live an extravagant lifestyle, which makes this little treat so much more enjoyable. The limo driver opens the car door for us and Pace gestures for me to get in first. I slid across the black leather seat, my eyes wandering around the dim interior of the car. There's soft jazz music playing, and a bottle of champagne chilling on ice. He's pulled out all the stops. The date hasn't even begun yet, and I'm already in love with it.

Pace slides in beside me, and I note the soft scent of aftershave permeating the air around him. I picture him taking extra care in getting ready, and I like it. I can't help my eyes falling to his lap, wondering if he's gone commando tonight like he so often does, or if

I'll find boxers underneath and be able to unwrap him like a present...

"My eyes are up here, angel," Pace reminds me with a playful smirk.

I grin back at him, unable to help the bubble of laughter that escapes me. "Sorry. I guess I'm just excited to be alone – just us."

"Me too. But you don't have to strip me naked and ride me in the limo, we have the whole night ahead of us."

While I lean back against the seat, feeling blissfully happy, Pace pops the cork on the champagne and pours us each a glass. I take a sip of the bubbly drink and make a little contented sound. Pace's eyes dance on mine as he takes a drink of his own. Then he presses his lips to mine. It's an innocent kiss – he's nuzzling into me and lightly kissing my mouth – but the promise of hot, wild sex later tonight hangs in the air between us.

"When are we going to have the discussion?" he asks, pulling back from his kisses.

"What discussion?" I ask.

He lifts one dark eyebrow and smirks at me. "About our living arrangements."

Oh. That one. We've had this argument probably ten times already, but couldn't seem to figure out where we were going to live, and what to do with each of our places. Pace wanted Max and I to move into his condo as soon as possible – yesterday preferably, but I was hanging on to my home. It was all Max knew. My office was already set up there, and I had a small backyard where Max could play. Besides, Pace's condo wasn't exactly baby-friendly.

"I have a solution," he says, bringing his lips to my neck.

"I'm listening," I say. I don't want another heated argument where we don't get anywhere. We're supposed to be enjoying tonight. And he knows where I stand, so if he suggests we move in to his condo again, I won't hesitate to put him in his place.

"What if I bought a new home for us? Somewhere with a home office for you, a backyard for Max, and an extra bedroom for baby number two."

I choke on my champagne. Fighting to clear my airway, I sputter and cough. "Baby number two?"

Pace smiles at me adoringly. "I want to get you pregnant."

I think my ovaries just melted. "What?"

"I think Max should have a little brother or sister, don't you?"

Dear God, what is he saying? My mouth opens, then closes, like a fish gasping for air. "Y-yes, someday, but we're not even married." Why I just said that, I have no idea. I'm smart enough to know that people don't have to be married to have a baby. Elan and I were never married, and Max is the best thing that's ever happened to me. Aside from Pace.

Pace just smiles knowingly at me. "I'm just saying, it might be a good idea to stop taking your birth control pills. We could pull the goalie, so to speak, and see what happens." The light flickering in his eyes tells me that he's secretly in love with this idea. A warm tingling sensation spreads through me. I don't know if it's the champagne, or the deep love and adoration I feel emanating from this beautiful man.

I'm so thrown off by him wanting another baby, I haven't even been able to process his statement about buying us a home. One thing at a time. "This new home idea," I say. "Tell me more."

"I'm thinking we each sell our places, and move into a new home that we pick out together."

His idea is actually a good one. Someplace fresh where we can both start over. And if we're looking ahead to the long term, room for another baby is probably a smart idea too. There is one thing that bugs me, though.

"When you said that *you* would buy us a home…I want to be in this fifty-fifty with you."

His mouth curls up in a grin. "So you're in?"

"I'm in. Except for the baby part, I've just barely lost the baby weight, so forgive me if I'm not jumping for joy at the thought of gaining another forty pounds and toting around a big belly, with a toddler on my hip." Plus Max is still in diapers. Maybe we can wait a little while, for my sanity's sake. Pace chuckles and I swat at his shoulder. "Why are you laughing?"

"I'm just picturing you barefoot and pregnant," he says, with a wide smile. "And I like it."

"You pig," I murmur, but I'm unable to hide my smile.

Pace moves closer and places his hand on my stomach. "I don't care how much weight you gain or lose, and for the record, I can't wait to see you with a big belly, knowing I put a life inside of you."

His words warm my heart, but before I have time to respond, the limo pulls to a stop. I glance out the heavily tinted windows and am surprised to see we're parked near a plane. "What's this?" I ask.

The limo driver parks and Pace opens the door. "Remember when I said we were going to have fun tonight?"

I nod.

"I meant all night. It's an overnight date. Lynn is staying the night with Max. We're headed to Napa Valley for a wine tasting and dinner, and a night alone in a hotel. Is that okay with you?"

"I...I..." The thought of staying an entire night alone with Pace is intoxicating.

"Max will be in good hands," he says. "And so will you."

I swallow and follow him from the limo to the jet, still in a state of shock.

"Is this a private plane?" I ask.

He nods. "It's Colton's."

"I don't have an overnight bag," I say, stopping at the stairs that lead to the jet.

"Already taken care of."

"You packed for me?" I ask, spinning to face him.

He meets my eyes. "I told you I would always take care of you."

I swallow as a sudden rush of emotion hits me. He's planned everything out so carefully tonight and just knowing the time and care he put into this date makes me weak in the knees. In everything he does, I can *feel* his love for me. It's not in his words, it's in his actions. It's always been that way, I realize.

After a short flight, with more champagne, and a delicious wine tasting where the sommelier paired fancy wines with scrumptious foods from the menu, we are full, happy, and slightly tipsy.

Pace and I spent most of dinner discussing which areas we would like to live and the features of our new dream home.

"Do you remember that night at the gala?" I ask, once we're back inside of yet another limo, this one taking us to our hotel for the night.

Pace's deep blue eyes have been on mine almost the entire night – and his attention is dizzying. "Of course. What about it?"

"You brought that terrible date." I giggle. Platinum blonde hair, large double-D breasts and not an ounce of fat or jiggle anywhere on her body.

He groans. "The date from hell," he agrees.

I recall how he spent a good portion of the evening talking to me, even though he was there with another woman. "Did you have sex with her that night?" I hadn't meant to ask that, but the words roll off my wine-loosened tongue before I can take them back.

"Do you really want to know?" he asks, his tone low.

I wince. Geez, maybe not. I give a careful nod.

Pace looks out the window, looking a little lost. "We didn't have intercourse." He doesn't say anything more, and I don't pry. I don't want to ruin this perfect evening with talk of our exes. I'm just feeling nostalgic about how much Pace has evolved from the man I first met.

I reach over and take his hand in mine. "I love you no matter what." We just recently started saying the L word to each other, and each time my belly does a happy little flip. "All the baggage in the world couldn't keep me from you. Besides, I have baggage of my own."

"Max is not baggage. He's a bonus. I've told you that." Pace brings my hand to his mouth and kisses the back of it, his eyes lingering on mine. "What I remember best about that night at the gala is how completely stunning and classy you were. The moment I saw you, my mouth went dry and I was at a loss for words. My heart started beating too damn fast and I had no idea what was happening. I think I fell in love with you right then."

I smirk. "I think you weren't used to a woman telling you no."

"Hell no I wasn't." He treats me to a gorgeous smile, the light, playful mood of this evening returning between us. His eyes linger on mine, turning serious. "Did you take your birth control pill yet today?" he asks.

"Pace!" I smack his shoulder again. "Yes. I did." I had no idea he'd want another baby so quickly. It's actually quite sweet. I can picture his big hands cradling a tiny newborn, and my chest feels tight. "But since I didn't pack my pills…" I grin.

Pace's answering smile is wide and lights up his entire face. Heaven help me, will I ever be able to say no to this man?

Our limousine stops and I see a beautiful hotel lit up against the dark sky.

Pace has called ahead and somehow, miraculously we are already checked in to a lavish hotel room that's more like a large apartment. There's a basket of toiletries, along with men's and women's pajamas sitting on a side table waiting for us. And an overnight bag that Pace says Sophie packed for me. Even though Colton's reaction to us dating wasn't great at first, he's come around, seeing that Pace is different with me.

I explore the suite – there's a living room outfitted with two cream-colored sofas and a glass coffee table between them, a huge marble bathroom with a steam shower and Jacuzzi tub and a bedroom with a fluffy king bed. It's too much for just one night, but I love that Pace has gone all out for our night away, knowing they are so rare.

"This is amazing," I say, turning to him. He's been quietly following me from room to room, clearly loving the joy on my face.

"I'm glad you like it, angel." We're standing in the bedroom, where the huge king bed looms in the distance. Spending the entire night with him in a bed will be a luxury. Even sex in an actual bed is a rarity for us. We're typically trying to hide from Max, and sex is generally quick and quiet. His office is an old favorite – bent over the desk, or sitting on top while he thrusts between my thighs. Tonight there will be no interruptions. No distractions. A warm shiver races over me as Pace's dark blue eyes roam over my exposed skin.

"Come here," he says, his voice low and authoritative.

My panties dampen instinctively at the rough sound of his voice. I walk slowly, seductively toward him, thankful without a clunky cast on my arm, I actually feel sexy. I stop in front of him, my high heels giving me an extra boost of height, so my lips are at his throat, and gaze up at him with soulful eyes.

He leans down, bringing his mouth to mine and kisses me, long and deep. I feel his hands skim carefully down my sides, until they find my backside and cup my ass cheeks, his fingers squeeze and a rough growl escapes his throat. His worshipful reverence of my body makes me feel like maybe I am enough, makes me feel like I should just forget about those last ten pounds and the extra jiggle and accept the woman I am now. I reach up and twine my fingers into the hair at the back of his neck, enjoying the way his roaming hands are exploring my body. While my tongue strokes his, Pace trails his hands down my ass until he reaches under my skirt and lifts my dress up around my waist. His warm palms meet bare skin and he smiles, looking down appreciatively at the black g-string I've worn tonight just for him.

"Hmm," he growls. "No boy shorts tonight?"

I almost chuckle, but instead I bite my lip while trying not to smile. He's never complained about my choice of comfy underwear, but I can tell he likes this sexier version I'm wearing tonight. I shrug. "Special occasion and all that." I almost want to tell him about the matching bra with its demi cups, but I know he'll discover that soon enough.

He runs one finger along the seam of my pussy, lingering over the sensitive nub, and sparks of heat lick at my inner muscles. Then he drops my skirt and his fingers move to the zipper at my back, slowly sliding it lower until I can step out of the dress.

As soon as I'm free of the dress, his dark eyes glaze over with lust and wandering hands are back, gently touching and appreciating every curve I have. I stand straight and tall in the black heels, feeling every bit like a powerful sex goddess.

Deciding he still has far too many clothes on, my fingers move to his belt buckle. His erection is already tenting his slacks, and I'm dying to feel his hot, hard flesh in my hands. Especially since I now have the use of both hands.

When we're both finally stripped of every last piece of clothing, we fall into bed in a tangle of limbs, hot mouths fused together and greedy hands roaming and exploring.

The first time we make love that night, it's with me on top, a position we've both come to love. His mouth is on my breasts and his hands are on my ass, and even though I'm on top, he's the one controlling each powerful thrust as his hips rock into me.

The second time, we're lying together in a spoon position, his arms curled around me and his mouth by my ear.

"I love you," he whispers.

Hearing him say those words means everything to me. Hearing him say them to Max the first time was nearly my undoing. I feel so connected to Pace, so in sync, and full of love.

"Show me," I whisper back. As sexually satisfying as our physical relationship is, once is never enough. I've come to appreciate his ability to go again and again. His stamina is just one of the many things about him I find incredibly sexy.

Pace's hand trails along my waist, moving lower until he reaches between my legs and begins to gently rub. "Are you sore?" he asks.

"No."

"Is this hot little cunt ready for me again?" he asks. I love the filthy things he whispers during sex. I feel myself growing wet.

With one hand parting my inner lips, the other begins lightly stroking my clit. The sudden rush of pleasure makes me cry out. I'm still sensitive from the last orgasm he gave me, and my body trembles involuntarily. I feel his cock hardening between my butt cheeks and I grind against him, desperate.

I reach between us, angling his cock to my opening and push back, taking in the broad head of him. He thrusts, slowly, lazily, as he continues rubbing me. When I come all over his cock, he finally enters me fully, brutally pounding into me again and again, as if the act of holding back had been killing him. The tight squeeze of my inner muscles makes him groan long and low.

"Fuck, angel. Go easy on me," he whispers against my hair.

His warm breath comes in fast pants against my ear and I close my eyes, loving the feel of his body enveloping mine. We're as close as two people can possibly be. Wrapping both arms around me, he pumps into me several more times before finally finding his release. He comes with a low groan, and I curl my legs to my chest, letting him hold me until his cock softens and we are both at that quiet, still moment just before sleep takes over.

I lay in his arms, reflecting on my life before Pace. It was chaotic and stressful at times. I was surviving as a single mother, doing the best I could. But now I feel more in control, happier, loved and cherished. And having a partner to lean on when I need it is such a comforting feeling. I am so thankful that I gave Pace a chance. Everything I knew about the young, wealthy bachelor told me to stay away, I'm just glad my heart did not listen. He means everything to me. And I know Max loves him just as much.

Epilogue

PACE

My life is so very different than it was just three short months ago, but I've never felt happier. Knowing there's a beautiful, strong woman in my life and a little boy depending on me to be the best man I can be – it's a powerful feeling. My life is so much fuller than it ever was before. I'm lucky and I know that.

We moved into our new home two months ago and Elan visits one Saturday a month. Max doesn't really know who he is, but he tolerates his presence and has even begun interacting with him, handing him toys and babbling at him. But for all intents and purposes, I am his father, a fact that makes me feel incredibly proud. I will be the one to teach him about sports and cars and women. But at this moment, there is only one woman on my mind.

"You have to help Papa," I say to Max, squaring his shoulders and looking down into his big blue eyes.

Max giggles and bounces up and down, seeming to understand the excitement of our secret game. I'm not nervous, the only thing making me sweat is that I just handed a three-carat diamond ring to an infant. I've been instructed to call Colt and Collins right after this, since they both know I'm popping the question today.

"Don't eat this, buddy," I say to Max solemnly. He has the ring around his thumb and peering down at it like it's a magical stone. Heck, maybe it is. This stone will turn us into an official family.

I can hear Kylie humming in the kitchen where she's making her homemade pasta sauce. She loves the kitchen in our new home and picked most of the features herself. From the large butcher-block island, to the dark cabinets, to the farm sink.

"Go give this to Mumma," I tell him and guide him by the shoulders from the family room.

Max toddles forward down the hall and I follow close behind him, unable to hide the smile on my lips. I'm excited and overwhelmed all at once.

Kylie's standing in front of the stove, stirring a pot of sauce on the range.

"Angel?" I ask.

She spins to face me and my heart trips over itself. Tendrils of hair have escaped from her ponytail and her pretty green eyes land on mine. All the doubt and worry that maybe I should have planned something big and extravagant fall away. This is exactly the way this moment is supposed to go. This is us. This is our life.

"Mumma," Max says, lifting the ring up for her to see.

Kylie's gaze leaves mine and lowers to Max. Her eyes get big and her hand flies up to her mouth.

"Pace?" she says, tears in her eyes.

I swallow back a wave of emotion. "Will you be mine?" I ask, fighting to keep the emotion from my voice.

She flings herself forward into my arms and I hold her securely to my chest. "Angel?" I ask while moisture swims in my eyes.

"Yes! Of course," she cries.

I reach down and grab Max, lifting him into my arms so we're all three hugging. Kylie is crying and Max looks concerned as he watches her, until we both start laughing and then his little mouth breaks into a wide smile.

When I slip the ring over her knuckle, my throat gets tight. I've never been this damn emotional, but these two bring out a totally different man in me. The man I've always wanted to be. Standing here, the three of us, in our new family home, I finally feel complete.

***

"Please, help yourself." Kylie sets the serving dish of pasta down in the center of the dining table, and I can't help but notice the way her eyes linger on her ring, turning it this way and that way to catch the light.

Colton and Sophie are sitting across the table, and Collins is by my side. He's alone and he seems distracted and somewhat somber, given the celebratory mood. When I ask him about Tatianna, his bombshell girlfriend who is rarely at his side, he gives a brief answer about her working tonight.

"So this is the famous pasta sauce Pace has bragged so much about," Colton says, serving Sophie a dish first, and then himself.

I couldn't resist inviting the whole family over after Kylie said yes, and of course they all came. Sophie hugging and crying with Kylie as the gushed over how beautiful her ring was. I felt proud in that moment.

"So, when's the big day?" Collins asks, gazing at me approvingly.

My eyes find Kylie's. We haven't discussed that yet, but I could already envision Max serving as my best man. "She's in charge." I nod toward Kylie.

She smiles at me adoringly. "I'm not sure. We're still getting settled into our new house, but I don't want to wait long."

I agree completely. In my view, there's no point in waiting. I want this woman to be my wife. And I want to adopt Max as my own, and give them both my last name. I approached Elan with this idea during his last visit, and while he didn't seem thrilled with the idea, he was open to it. He knows they are my family and doesn't want to stand in the way of that.

After dinner, Max entertains us all by dancing in the living room, then streaking naked through the house when Kylie tries to change him into pajamas. There is never a dull moment here, not like at my old bachelor pad. When I reflect on my life before, I really can't fathom why I wasted so many years pursing meaningless flings. I guess because I was waiting for the right woman to come along. My eyes connect with Kylie's as she hoists Max up onto her hip. She is my everything.

"Goodnight, guys, I'm going to get Max to bed," she says.

I jog over to where they're standing in the hallway. I wrap them both in my arms, appreciating the soft feel of Max's cheek against my neck, and the scent of Kylie's delicate skin warming me. After he's asleep, there will be drinks and music and celebration for our engagement, but in this moment, there is just me and the two who own my heart in a darkened hallway. I press my lips to Max's forehead. "*Goodnight, Moon,*" I whisper. He yawns and rests his head against Kylie's shoulder. I kiss Kylie's lips and stroke her cheek. "I love you," I say, my voice getting tight.

"I love you, Pace," she whispers back.

I find her hand in the darkness and give it a squeeze, loving the solid feel of the ring decorating her finger. Sometimes I'm overcome with emotion for no reason at all. Imagining Max as a grown man, myself and Kylie with silver in our hair, still just as in love as we are today. There is so much ahead of us in this beautiful life, so much to look forward to.

"I'm going to put our son to bed," she whispers against my lips, giving me another kiss. "Be right back."

Our son.

A wife and a son...who would have thought? A lazy smile tugs at my mouth as I watch her carry him down the hall toward his bedroom. I am one lucky son of a bitch.

***

Author's Note

Thank you for reading! When I began Filthy Beautiful Lies, I knew Colton had two gorgeous brothers, and while I never dreamed I'd be giving them each their own story, readers asked and I just couldn't resist spending more time with the Drake brothers.

That is how Pace and Kylie came to be. It probably didn't hurt that I also have a 13-month old son at home, and so Max's mannerisms, personality and even the sign language were all taken from my personal life.

I hope you enjoyed this story of second chance love, and will stick around for FILTHY BEAUTIFUL FOREVER, coming January 12, 2015.

Filthy Beautiful Forever

The final book in the Filthy Beautiful Lies series

Collins Drake exercises control over all facets of his life. From his business, to satisfying his physical needs … it all happens on his command.

So when a woman shows up at his door and reminds him of a promise they made each other when they were just ten years old, it shouldn't have the ability to rock his entire world.

Yet it does.

Because Mia Monroe wasn't just his childhood best friend, she wasn't just the girl he lost his virginity to and hasn't seen since, she's the one exception to his perfect control. And piece by piece, she's about to tear apart his carefully laid plans.

Tell Me Your Favorite Part!

If you enjoyed Filthy Beautiful Lust, I invite you to head over to the retailer where you purchased it and let me know which part was your favorite. Reading reviews is often the highlight of my day, plus they help new readers discover the book. I thank you in advance!

Connect With Kendall Ryan:

http://www.kendallryanbooks.com
http://www.facebook.com/kendallryanbooks
http://www.twitter.com/kendallryan1

Also By Kendall Ryan:

Unravel Me
Make Me Yours
Resisting Her
Hard to Love
Working It
Craving Him
All or Nothing
When I Break
When I Surrender
When We Fall

CPSIA information can be obtained at www.ICGtesting.com
Printed in the USA
LVOW07s2125201016

509597LV00013B/1210/P